Chesstise

Khaliyl Adisa

Khaliyl Lee-Adisa

I appreciate the
support and love thank you
Ms. Coco-Chanel! Blessings!

Printed in the United States of America

First Printing, 2016

ISBN: 978-1-5356-0139-9

Contents

1

THE MARRIAGE BED IS UNDEFILED

"I now pronounce you Mr. and Mrs. Jacobson," announced Bishop Nelson. Having been before asked to do so, Mr. Roman Jacobson clutched his bride and kissed her deeply. Joyce Jacobson felt her toes tingle when her husband embraced her tightly and eagerly kissed her. She was always infatuated by his warm, amorous smooches. It was an indication that he loved her wholeheartedly and would never be replaced.

"Whoop, whoop!" The guests shouted, hollered, whistled, and clapped, breaking the trance that the couple was engulfed in.

"Congratulations," whispered Bishop Nelson in Roman's right ear.

"Thank you, sir," Roman replied as a smile lit up his whole face. Roman grabbed his wife's hand and quickly led her down the aisle toward the main exit. The guests who were now on their feet cheered loudly which echoed throughout the sanctuary halls of North Central Church of God in Christ.

"I know that's right!!" shouted a Southern female voice as the couple darted through the front doors where their limousine driver awaited.

"Congratulations Mr. and Mrs. Jacobson," said the limo driver as he opened the car door for the couple to enter.

"Thank you," Joyce said as she positioned herself comfortably in the silky, caramel colored leather seats. The limo driver gently closed the door behind the groom and hurried to the driver's seat. Roman reveled in the moment he was in and exhaled loudly. "Wow baby, look at all of this," Joyce said in amazement. The limousine was decorated and arranged with expensive champagne, assorted chocolates, and rose petals.

"So are we going to make the most of this now or wait for the hotel?" asked Roman in a deep, low sexy voice. Joyce, who sat across from Roman, raised her left eyebrow and crossed her legs.

"You were gonna make me wait for the hotel," Joyce said, smiling slyly. The limousine engine came to life but was drowned out by the cheers that made their way from inside the church next to the limo. Roman and Joyce waved as the limo slowly pulled away from the curb. However, among all the smiles and grins one face stood out vaguely. An elderly man with a cane wearing an expensive jet black tuxedo glared at the limo. The cane the man gripped tightly was unique and fascinating looking. It had designs of chess pieces all over the frame along with the handle being shaped as the king. His expression was hard mixed with a look of disgust.

"Who frowns at the sight of marriage?" Roman wondered.

"Who is that?" Joyce asked pointing at the old man.

"I don't know. I'm not sure he was invited," Roman replied.

"Well why is he looking like he's got a problem?" Joyce asked angrily as she pushed the button to lower the window.

"What're you 'bout to do?" Roman asked.

"See what his problem is," answered Joyce.

"Joy, baby, no!" This is our day. We're not gonna let nobody ruin it," Roman said reassuringly. Joyce smiled and kissed her hubby.

"I love when you call me Joy," she whispered in his ear.

Roman looked his angelic wife over and bit his bottom lip. She wore a black lingerie nightgown with sexy black open-toed heels revealing nicely red-polished, pedicured toes that made her look exquisite. Her light, mocha colored skin was glowing in the midst of the apple cinnamon candle's light. Joyce was a sexy redbone with long silky black hair and curly jet black eyelashes that complemented her face. Still the most striking feature about Joyce's face was her lovely hazel eyes. Whenever he met her gaze it was as if he were looking in the windows of heaven. Roman remained mesmerized only momentarily. This was the first time he had seen her or any woman in a bra-and-panties nightgown and he couldn't wait any longer to have her. He marveled at her cleavage and noticed her nipples hardening. Her 34D-sized bosom looked great in her Victoria Secret push up bra. "I can't wait to suck on those," Roman breathed. He walked his six-foot-tall muscular frame toward his beautiful wife. Before he could touch her she submitted to her husband and dropped to her knees. She felt she had no choice but to surrender to Roman. He was a tall, dark, handsome man with broad shoulders, chiseled chest, thick biceps, and a ripped midsection that was covered with abs. Joyce felt her pussy getting soaking wet as she looked her husband over. All he wore were Calvin Klein boxers that had a thick bulge in the center. She slowly pulled his boxers down his sturdy legs and revealed a thick, dark, twelve-inch penis that stood at full attention.

"Oh my," Joyce gasped as her eyes widened. Her vagina twitched at the sight of Roman's manhood. This made her crave Roman even more and she didn't hesitate to take what was rightfully hers. Joyce grabbed her husband's long, thick, dark tool and slowly began stroking. Roman's breathing intensified as he looked intently at his wife who reciprocated with a seductive stare. She licked the head of his penis and swirled her tongue in circular motions that surely teased him.

"Aww, baby," he whispered. His eyes rolled in the back of his head as Joyce proceeded to lick the base of his shaft while massaging his scrotum. She alternated between licking the head and the base of the penis. "There you go. Don't stop," Roman whispered. Joyce then took his scrotum in her mouth and began humming on his testicles. This put Roman on the threshold of pleasure and pain. "Aaagghh!!" he cried out from the intense sensational feeling.

"Mm," she moaned. His cries turned her on even more and she eagerly accepted her husband's foot-long offering down her throat. Roman shuddered as Joyce deep throated his cock and moved her mouth up and down his thick shaft. Every time she came up near the thick, bulbous head of the penis she swirled and sucked hard to intensify the pleasure. "Umm, baby!! I can't hold it!!" He grabbed his wife's long strands of silky, black hair and held her still and banged her vocal cords. Gurgling and gagging noises were the only responses coming from Joy. Roman's facial expression became more serious as he strived for his release. His buttocks squeezed together and his posture became more vertical, shifting on his feet from flat-footed to on the balls of his feet. "Baby...I'm 'bout to cum!!" He yelled and exploded his thick warm semen down her throat.

"Yum." Joyce looked up at her husband and smiled warmly. Roman's breathing slowly subsided.

"Whoa," he said staring at his now flaccid penis. "That was the most intense feeling I ever felt."

"Mm-hmm, cause I'm your woman and I got you," Joyce said. Roman bent down to his submissive wife and in one swift movement he lifted her and placed her on the bed. He hadn't noticed his surroundings as a result of paying so much attention to Joyce. The expensive decorated queen-sized bed was covered in glittery red rose petals. Beside the bed toward the left stood an antique dresser with a Krug Clos d'Ambonnay champagne bottle open and ready for the couple. Next to the champagne bottle were two wine glasses with each of their names engraved in them.

"This is beautiful," he said in amazement.

"I know baby and we deserve it," Joyce replied.

"Lay down," Roman said in a strong masculine voice.

"Ooh, okay daddy," Joyce whispered. She melted whenever Roman spoke to her like that. She always was the type of woman that wanted to be dominated and put her in place. She never submitted to a man that couldn't handle her. Joyce went to take her panties off but Roman kept her still and effortlessly ripped them off. "Ohh," she cried. Roman's aggressive, take-charge demeanor was more than she bargained for. He parted her thighs, lowered his head, and slid his tongue along her voluptuous pussy lips. "Mmmm," Joyce moaned and her hazel eyes rolled to the back of her head. He licked her down with his long tongue along with sliding his middle finger in and out her wet pussy. "Oh God! That so feels so good," she screamed squirming in pleasure. Roman then feverishly lapped the juices oozing from her swollen pussy and sucked her clitoris. "Oh, God! Don't stop!" she screamed. Her whole body began to tremble and shake as he licked her rapidly. A surge of pleasure rushed through her entire body as she climaxed. "Ohh, ohh, ohh!" She couldn't process anything except how good it felt. Roman moved his head from her moist, pulsating haven and positioned himself missionary style over his wife. He yanked Joyce's black push up bra from her chest and proceeded in sucking her hard, gumdrop nipples. His tongue explored every crevice of her breasts and neck. Tingling sensations surged throughout Joyce's body as Roman sucked, licked, and nibbled at her nipples and neck. "Mmm, baby," Joyce whispered. Her swollen pussy was soaking wet and throbbing from the sensation she received from his tongue. She wrapped her legs around his waist, inviting his manhood to enter her juicy wet pussy. Roman smiled at his wife as he slowly slid his hardened penis into her slippery vaginal opening. She gasped as he stretched her to new widths. "Oh!!" she cried, eyes widening. Roman felt her vaginal walls separate since she was so tight. He slowly pumped in and out of her while massaging her breasts. She focused on his physical and emotional ardor. She squealed and moaned in delight and pleasure. Roman sucked her neck but stopped frequently to survey her elegant facial expressions. Looking at her made him really want to give it to her. His thrusting motion changed from slow to a fast, long stroking rhythm. "Aaagghh!!" Joyce cried grabbing for his back and digging her manicured nails into his skin. She moaned loudly as he shoved his foot-long penis in and out of her rapidly. "Oh! Oh! Oh! I'm 'bout to nut!!" she screamed loudly. A wave of intense pleasure and ecstasy came over her as she exploded around his cock. Roman accelerated his strokes, found her G spot, and kept hitting it. "Oh,

God! This is your pussy, daddy, it's yours!" she yelled. Her screams and cries boosted his ego and elevated the sensation he was feeling. He grabbed Joyce's hair tightly and shot his sperm inside his beautiful wife.

"I love you Joy," he breathed in her ear.

"I love you too, baby," she replied. She rubbed and caressed his backside until they both fell asleep in the missionary position they made love in.

2
BLACKMAIL

Joyce Jacobson awoke in a pleasantly splendid mood. She smiled and inhaled deeply, reminiscing on what took place last night. She looked over at her husband who obviously had moved from the position they fell asleep in. Her husband had a very attractive face that could easily be on a cover of a male magazine. Roman had a low cut fade and nicely trimmed sideburns that connected to his goatee. His lips, however, were the most striking feature because they were thick and juicy and fit his mouth perfectly. Joyce leaned toward her sleeping husband and kissed his sexy lips. Roman must have been exhausted because he didn't even budge. "I love you, baby," she whispered to her unconscious husband. She then got up from the queen-sized bed naked and headed toward the bathroom. To her surprise the bathtub was already filled up with red glittery rose petals floating on the water. *"I guess we were supposed to use this,"* Joyce thought to herself. She dipped her hand in the water and felt it was still warm. This was not a shock to her because she knew the wealth that came with marrying Roman. This was an expensive hotel that provided great customer service and frequently checked the rooms to make sure clients' needs were met.

Joyce left the bathtub how she found it contemplating how lovely it would be to make love to Roman in it. She smiled as she envisioned the sexual possibilities that could be done inside the warm Jacuzzi bathtub. "Mm," she moaned softly to herself. She walked toward the right of the spacious bathroom passing the sink and stepped inside the shower. The glass door was already open as if it had already been prepared to invite her in. A bar of soap, Caress body wash, hair conditioner, and red washrags were already available in the shower. Joyce turned the knob toward hot and only had to wait momentarily for the water to warm up. She closed her eyes as the warm water hit her face and the rest of her body. "Ooh this water feels good," she whispered to herself. She retrieved a Caress body wash, opened it, and squeezed a large amount in her palm. She placed the body wash on the shelf where she found it and began cleansing herself. Next, she took the hair conditioner removed the cap and poured it on her head. After returning the conditioner to the shelf she ran her fingers through her hair and washed herself from head to toe. While washing herself she thought once again about the sex that she had with her husband and gave in to the masturbating urge. She rotated her fingers back and forth rapidly against her clit. Her eyes rolled to the back of her head as she quickly climaxed and squirted inside the shower stall. "Mm," she moaned softly and grabbed a red rag that was neatly hung up. She held it under the water and retrieved the body wash again. She opened the bottle poured about an ounce on her rag and put the bottle back. She cleansed herself good this time, focusing on her vaginal area. She rinsed herself off and turned the knob until the water stopped running. She stepped out the stall and reached for a red towel that was folded on a stand. Joyce dried herself off quickly and wrapped the towel around her hair leaving her body bare and exposed. She stood in front of the sink and wiped the mirror thus revealing her gorgeous reflection. She noticed the toothpaste, Colgate mouthwash, and red toothbrushes. She picked up the toothbrush and toothpaste and unfastened the cap. She squeezed the mint green paste on the toothbrush bristles and then began brushing. Joyce took exceptional care of her straight white teeth and healthy pink gums. Joyce brushed in circles and never forgot to brush her tongue. She spit out the white paste while turning on the faucet for water. Joyce then picked up the Colgate mouthwash, unscrewed the cap, poured the blue green mouthwash inside the cap, filled her mouth, and began swishing. She did so for about two minutes before spitting and rinsing her mouth out with water. "Ring, Ring!!" the doorbell chimed in throughout their lavish hotel room. Joyce opened a cabinet and a removed a pair of pink bed slippers matched with a pink robe. She undid the towel around her head as she walked out the bathroom toward the front door. Joyce opened the door and was greeted by a handsome young Italian man. Despite being in a mail delivery uniform it was not difficult to see that he was muscular and well built. *"He's cute,"* Joyce thought to herself as she smiled warmly.

"Ciao, Mrs. Jacobson," greeted the Italian man. "I have a package sent to you by priority mail," he said as he handed Joyce a long, thick beige envelope. "I just need your signature right here," he added handing her an electronic pad also. Joyce signed the electronic device and handed it back to the young man. "Thank you, adios Mrs. Jacobson," he said as he turned to walk away. Joyce closed the door behind her and sat on top of the lid of the toilet seat. She ripped open the large envelope and pulled out a smaller beige envelope with her name engraved in gold letters. However, the mail did not show who it was sent from. She opened the envelope with her eyebrows raised retrieved a small letter unfolded it and read:

Dear Joyce Jacobson,

I know everything about you and what your true motives are. Everything you have done in the dark will finally come to light. Your lies and secrets will be exposed. Your past has come back to haunt you. In seven days you must return to the church you got married in to determine your future. I warn you that failure to comply will result in deadly consequences.

Sincerely, I hope you enjoyed your honeymoon.

What the hell is this?" Joyce said to herself. Her heart raced and her face got warm. She became agitated and distraught. This was the most disturbing thing she'd ever read and it made her emotionally disoriented. She looked inside the larger torn envelope and pulled out Kodak film pictures. She went through pictures and her jaw dropped. "Oh my god," she said softly. Instantly she felt sick and nauseous. She threw the pictures on the floor, got up, lifted the toilet seat, and threw up. "Uuggh," she exhaled and flushed yellow-orange vomit down the toilet. She slowly got up and staggered toward the sink and washed her face with warm water. "*Who sent this?*" Joyce thought to herself. She rinsed out her mouth and then dried off her face with the towel that was previously wrapped around her head. She turned and looked down at the photos and winced at the sight. Reluctantly, she knelt down, picked up the letter, photos, and envelope, and sat on the toilet lid. Joyce, who was now perplexed and bewildered, stared at the words on the letter. She could not understand how anyone was capable of sending this and remaining anonymous. To make matters worse the sender apparently knew a great deal about her past, something she locked away and buried years ago. Fear immobilized Joyce and kept her paralyzed in her thoughts. She felt immensely threatened that her marriage could possibly be at great risk by this unknown sender. Roman was the man of her dreams who solved all her financial problems and personal dilemmas. She would do whatever it took to keep her past hidden until she accomplished what she sought out to achieve. She had no choice but to follow the letter's instructions and retreat back to the church where she'd become betrothed. She headed for the kitchen, crumpling up the letter and photos as she walked, and threw them in a disposable bin before she sat on a stool by the kitchen counter. Joyce surveyed the hotel room and fixed her eyes on her unconscious husband and sighed. *"Rome, you're a good man,"* she thought to herself. She then noticed two suitcases near the edge of the queen-sized bed. Instantly she knew which luggage contained her outfits. She got off the stool, walked toward the Louis Vuitton suitcase, picked it up and gently placed it on the bed. She quietly unzipped the suitcase in regards of her sleeping husband. Joyce opened her suitcase, which revealed neatly folded jeans, shirts, and blouses in the center compartment. Black socks and pantyhose were assorted in the upper half of the suitcase. A variety of panties and bras of every color accompanied her socks. Joyce moved her jeans to the side and retrieved an aloe vera and cocoa butter lotion bottle. She let the bathrobe around her body drop to the floor. Joyce unfastened the cap and squeezed the bottle of oozing, slimy, moist lotion in her palm. She rubbed her hands together and applied the lotion to her thin arms and slender body. After moisturizing the upper half of her body and torso she squeezed more lotion on herself and caressed her lovely legs and feet. Joyce placed the lotion bottle back into the suitcase and unzipped the upper half that contained her panties, bras, and socks. She pulled out a Victoria Secret push up bra and a G-string. Joyce stretched the G-string and slid them up her legs until it fit snugly around her waistline. Next, she clipped together the back of the bra, brought it over her head, and adjusted it until it was firmly around her plump 34D breasts. She moved her melons around a few times, making sure she felt comfortable within the bra. She then picked up some navy blue jeans and laid them on the bed several feet away from her husband. She picked up the jeans from the bed and put them on. The jeans hugged her hips and thighs and complimented her shape. She then thoroughly looked through her shirts, and pulled out a purple V-neck blouse. Joyce knew she would be showing off deep cleavage by wearing the blouse. She smiled to herself and put the purple blouse over her sexy body. Joyce looked ravishing although she wasn't finished preparing herself to be presentable. She sat down on the bed next to the suitcase and pulled out a pair of glittery, dark purple lavender Christian Louboutin closed-toe heels. She placed them on the ground and slid them on. They fit perfectly on her feet and felt smooth and comfortable. She got up off the bed, closed the suitcase and zipped it tightly. Joyce then unzipped a small pouch on the front side of the suitcase and pulled out a makeup kit with a mirror attached. She opened the kit, which revealed black eyeliner and mascara and different color shades of eye shadow. She picked up the black Maybelline mascara, untwisted it open, and while looking at the mirror she curled and darkened her eyelashes. Joyce was adept at making her eyes look stunning, and after careful observation she was satisfied. She then picked up an eye shadow brush and applied a hint of purple on her eyelids. After the finishing touches Joyce looked marvelous in the mirror as she made a bit of a conceited expression. Joyce quickly put her makeup and belongings in her kit and closed it. She returned the kit back into the front of the suitcase and zipped it. She then lifted the suitcase off the bed quietly and put it in an upright position beside her husband's. Joyce stared at Roman before she departed. "Nothing is gonna ruin this," she said to herself in a determined manner. With her heels on, Joyce click-clacked her way to the door and left gently, closing the door behind her. Joyce made her way downstairs to the main lobby of the hotel where reservations were made.

"Good morning, Mrs. Jacobson, how can I help you?" asked the female receptionist.

"I need a ride to the airport immediately and a flight to Atlanta," Joyce replied.

"Yes ma'am, right away." The receptionist typed some information in the laptop on her desk. "You're all set. A limousine is already available outside." The receptionist smiled warmly.

"Thank you," Joyce said.

"Oh will your husband be accompanying you, Mrs. Jacobson?" asked the receptionist.

"No we're leaving separately, thank you," Joyce replied hurriedly as she click-clacked her way toward the limousine outside.

3
BREAKING AND ENTERING

Detective Xavier Matthews volunteered to be on duty for the Atlanta, Georgia State Penitentiary visitation shift. He already had a case that involved a possible break-in at a nearby post office. Due to being the only African American in his agency he usually was obligated to take petty cases and mandatory prison guard shifts. He leaned forward in his chair behind the desk window and texted his colleague about the upcoming case. Xavier was anxious to finish his shift so he could begin his work in solving the post office break-in. The chief of police promised him a better law enforcement detective position if he could solve a difficult case by himself. Xavier's attention was suddenly diverted by an ebony redbone that walked up to his window.

"I'm here to visit someone," she said.

"Good afternoon, ma'am. I'll need your driver's license and you must sign this visitation form," he replied handing her the form to fill out. The woman complied with his instructions and handed him her driver's license and retrieved the form she was required to complete. Detective Matthews waited patiently for the woman to successfully sign the form as he entered her driver's license information in his computer. She hurriedly filled in the blanks of the visitation form as if it were something she was familiar with signing. She returned the form back to the officer who reviewed it and entered the data into his computer. "Okay, Ms. Jenkins walk down this hall and make a left. I will meet you at the door and let you in." Ms. Jenkins strutted her sexy body down the blue hallway, turned left, and stopped a few feet away from a metal detector and two double doors. Detective Matthews came through the double doors with a plastic container and walked toward Ms. Jenkins. "Ma'am, place all your personal belongings and metal objects in this bin then head through the metal detector. She did as she was instructed and placed her pocketbook in the bin and proceeded through the metal detector, and it did not trigger the alarm indicator. "Is this your first time here?" Detective Matthews asked.

"No," she replied.

"Okay, well no need to go over the facility's policies and procedures then. The guard in there will inform you on how much time you have left," he informed.

"Thank you," she said walking through the double doors that opened automatically for her. She stopped hesitantly then scanned the room where inmates were preoccupied with visiting relatives and loved ones. In the far right corner sat a dark-skinned man in a red and white striped jumpsuit who stared hard in her direction. Ms. Jenkins reluctantly walked in the direction of the dark-skinned man and slowly took a seat directly across from him. She stared at the man whose expression still remained hard, eyes narrowed, teeth clenched, and jaw muscles tightened.

"What took you so long?" the man asked in a deep gruff voice.

"I was busy, baby," she answered in a soothing voice. The man kissed his teeth and mumbled under his breath. Ms. Jenkins rolled her eyes. "What's wrong, Lorenzo?" She asked with a small hint of concern.

"Why don't you write me no more?" Lorenzo replied angrily. Ms. Jenkins ignored his exacerbated manner and slowly became annoyed with his questions.

"Are you mad?" Look I set up an appointment to see our son. Is that a problem?" she asked in an exasperated tone. Lorenzo's facial muscles relaxed as he examined Ms. Jenkins closely.

"You look good, Toya," he complimented.

"Glad you noticed," she replied sharply. Her appearance and demeanor were slowly beginning to arouse Lorenzo. "I missed you, bae," Lorenzo said in a low, deep voice.

"Mm-hmm, so far you're doing a good job showing it."

He reached for her right hand. "You know I love you. I'ma make everything good when I get out," he reassured. Lorenzo glanced at the clock that posted the time above the exit doors. "We got five minutes," he told her signaling for the security guard. They both got up from the table and followed the guard outside to a vacant armored truck. "Five minutes," the guard said as the two entered the armored vehicle and were locked in. Toya quickly noticed how spacious the truck was, but before she had time to observe her surroundings further Lorenzo grabbed her and began unbuttoning her skin-tight jeans.

"*He only complimented me once so far,*" she thought to herself as she took off her purple, glittery open-toed heels. Lorenzo quickly helped her out her jeans and then pulled his red jumpsuit pants down, exhibiting his dark erect penis. Toya leaned toward him for a kiss but her attempt was thwarted as he grabbed her forcefully and spun her around so that her backside faced his front, "*He won't even kiss me.*" Lorenzo spat in his right hand and moistened his erect penis with the slimy saliva as he bent Toya over with his left hand. Toya obliged and got in the position he wanted, spread her legs and touched her ankles. Lorenzo pulled Toya's panties to the side and rubbed the bulbous head of the penis in a circular motion against her clit to stimulate her pussy. Lorenzo did not seem to be very concerned with the way Toya was dressed or the scent of perfume that filled the truck. The position that he wanted her in indicated that he had no intent of looking at her beautiful face that she'd touched up with makeup. It was difficult for Toya to get sexually aroused due to the lack of foreplay and attentiveness. Lorenzo thrust his hard dick into Toya's semi-moist pussy and rammed her from behind without any remorse. "Oww!!" Toya cried out in pain. "*Really!! This is how he wanna do me,*" Toya continued to think and contemplate to herself. She was not mentally there and physically seemed resistant to Lorenzo. However, Lorenzo continued to puncture her with his dick, striving for his release. He grabbed a handful of Toya's hair as he jackhammered her pussy, ignoring her cries of pain. He smacked her right butt cheek.

"Yeah girl, who pussy this is?" Lorenzo said, raising his deep voice. Toya remained silent, closed her eyes, and waited for Lorenzo to ejaculate, which seemed like it would take an eternity. She was only going through the motions and felt no pleasure out of this sexual encounter. Lorenzo's breathing escalated and the grip he had around Toya's hair tightened. "Damn! I'm 'bout to bust in yo' pussy!" he yelled as he exploded inside of her like a fire hydrant. He filled her with his thick, hot sperm and stayed inside her for a moment longer, breathing rapidly.

"Finished?" Toya asked.

"Yeah, I'm straight," he replied slowly backing away from her, removing his penis from her, and pulling up his jumpsuit. A knock on the armored truck door indicated that the visitation time had expired. "Look, just stick to the plan until I get out and then we can get our son back," he said, walking toward the truck door. Toya had already slid her jeans up and was sliding into her closed-toe heels. They both exited the truck together, accompanied by the guard who escorted them back to the visitation room. The guard then turned toward Lorenzo and began restraining him with manacles, which was a standard procedure for inmates to undergo when departing after visitation. Toya stood only a few feet away, facing Lorenzo. "I only got a couple days left. Everything gonna be good when I'm out," he reiterated reassuringly.

The guard led him back to his cell. Toya remained in the same spot bewildered. "*He put me through all this and can't say that he loves me,*" Toya thought to herself. She watched as Lorenzo was being hauled back to his individual solitary confinement and though his last statement was partly true, he failed to notice her tears of disappointment and anguish. She turned to leave the visitation room and headed toward the double doors through which she entered. Toya was reunited with the same officer who previously checked her in at the front desk.

"Are you all set, Ms. Jenkins?" Toya nodded her head and was escorted outside the police department, accompanied by Detective

Matthews. "Have a nice day, ma'am," Detective Matthews said as Toya departed away from the police station without replying to the officer.

Oblivious to the fact Toya did not respond, Detective Matthews was overjoyed that his shift had ended and he could finally make his way to the post office. Xavier clocked out of his shift and quickly exited the police station. He made his way to his 2014 black-on-black z28 Chevy Camaro. Coincidentally, the break-in occurred a few blocks away from the police station, so fortunately Xavier would arrive there momentarily. Xavier entered his sports car and thrust his keys in ignition, bringing his vehicle to life as the engine roared. His Camaro was light, fast, and nimble with the ability to drive at optimal performance with the modifications that matched it to a race car. It had a powerful LS7 V8 engine capable of producing five hundred five horsepower with six-speed manual transmission, advanced suspension components, carbon ceramic brakes, and top-level aerodynamics. The interior of the vehicle was smooth black leather and had a strong smell of cologne due to the way Xavier prepared himself to be presentable to the women in his life. He bobbed and weaved through traffic as he sped way above the speed limit, and in a matter of minutes Xavier arrived at his destination. Upon his arrival he could already see the "do not enter" caution-strip line around the post office area. Xavier was dressed in casual clothes but he still had a credible reputation and colleagues ranked under him who were present at the post office. He opened the driver's side door and walked coolly to where the police crime scene investigators gathered around the crime scene to collect information. Detective Xavier Matthews spoke to the manager while his colleagues wrote down reports from the other two employees.

"How could someone break into a post office undetected?" asked the manager. Detective Matthews glanced at the woman's name tag which read Maria Sanchez and then looked at her left hand.

"Ms. Sanchez, the only explanation is that whoever did this hacked into the surveillance system which gave him or her enough time to access any confidential records," replied Detective Matthews.

"I understand that, detective, but we have security on duty while we're open, and twenty-four hour surveillance," Ms. Sanchez replied.

"Don't worry Ms. Sanchez, we'll catch them," said Detective Matthews with a reassuring smile. One of Detective Matthews's colleagues walked over and handed him a clipboard.

"Everything documented, sir," said the officer.

"I need the security camera tapes, names, and addresses of everyone who dropped off or received any mail, along with all the staff that worked in the past four days," said Detective Matthews.

"Yes, sir," replied the officer.

"Guess you're going to be very busy for the next few days," asked Ms. Sanchez smiling. Detective Matthews studied the appearance of Ms. Sanchez closely. She was a pleasantly plump Hispanic woman, probably in her early thirties. She seemed to take exceptional care of herself and looked financially stable. Ms. Sanchez stood approximately five feet seven inches tall with wide hips and large breasts. This Hispanic brunette had a cute round face with juicy glossy lips and dark brown eyes with no makeup. Detective Matthews smiled back in return while reaching in his back pocket.

"If you have any questions or concerns about the case here's my card. My cell is on there," he said smiling slyly.

"Okay, thank you," she replied. Detective Matthews walked over to his colleague who gathered all the materials he requested.

"Got everything?" Xavier asked. The officer nodded.

"Yes sir," he answered.

"All right, wrap this up. I'll review the evidence in my office." Detective Matthews took the folder and security tapes from the officer, walked to his Camaro, and entered the vehicle. The engine roared to life and Xavier sped all the way to the Atlanta Police Station and as soon as he arrived, he gathered all his belongings for the case and walked into the building. Xavier walked immediately to his office and shoved the security camera disc from the post office in a combination DVD and Blu-Ray player. He then sat down at his desk and watched the screen play the DVD. While examining the footage, Xavier opened the folder to review the information of all the clients and mail that were handled around the time of the incident. So far nothing appeared suspicious which was very common in his line of work. Suddenly, there was a knock at the door. "Come in," said Xavier without taking his eyes off the screen.

"Mr. Matthews would you like some coffee?" Xavier looked toward his office door and saw a Caucasian redhead woman, her long hair styled in a bun, wearing a gray matching business suit.

"Oh, good afternoon, Laura. Yes, I would like decaf please," he replied. Laura nodded and shut the door behind her as she left. Xavier's eyes darted back toward the screen and he focused intently on each person entering and leaving the post office. Every individual was dressed casual and portrayed no signs of malicious motives or intentions. Nothing seemed to be out of place at the moment but fortunately for Xavier he was very patient. He looked over the names and addresses of the mail that were sent out in the last few days but still there was nothing unusual. There were only two letters that were addressed overseas, which were for Adam Mitchel, and Joyce Jacobson. Xavier fast-forwarded the footage hoping to speed up the process of seeing something suspicious. However, his attention was diverted when Laura returned with his steamy, hot coffee.

"Here you go detective," Laura said, putting the cup of coffee on his desk.

"Thank you," Xavier said.

"You're welcome," she replied as she left Xavier's office. Xavier rewound the DVD back a few seconds then pushed play. Xavier picked up the coffee mug and took a sip of the decaffeinated coffee and burned his upper lip. "Ugh!" He made a low grunting sound and placed the mug back on his desk. He was eager to see anything suspicious unfold that would give him his first piece to solving this puzzle. Another civilian entered the post office with a package in hand. This particular individual was a middle-aged black male with a low-cut fade and stood approximately six feet even. He wore navy blue, neatly pressed jeans, a red-collared polo shirt, and black tennis shoes. The black man stopped at an area that was convenient and suitable for preparing mail to be delivered, which was exactly what he looked to be doing. After the black man filled out addressee information, he began placing stamps on the right hand corner of the brown package. "*Still nothing,*" Xavier thought to himself. He remained sedulous and paid close attention to the footage hoping for a sign of a clue. Suddenly, his attention was once again thwarted––this time by his cellular device vibrating. Xavier quickly snatched his cell phone out of his case that was clipped to the right side of his belt. He looked at his cell phone and saw a text from a familiar number. He touched the messaging app icon on his Blackberry Z3 to review the text message from Rosario. The text read: "Hey baby are u busy?"

Xavier smirked as he hastily began writing his reply. He tapped the send icon after he was through typing and his response read: "How are u. I'm not 2 busy at the moment wassup?" Xavier placed his phone on his office desk beside his coffee mug. Just as he was about to focus his attention back to the footage, his cell vibrated again. "Damn, that was fast," he said to himself as he retrieved his phone.

He tapped the message which read: "I'm off 2day and I cooked will u be stopping by?" Xavier chuckled to himself and stared at the winking face emoticon that came alongside the text. He thought about the possibilities that could occur tonight if he joined Rosario for dinner. She was mixed––Hispanic, Dominican, and Egyptian–– and performed things in the bedroom porn stars dreamed of.

Xavier responded to her invitation: "I'd love 2 join u. What u cook?" After Xavier sent out that text he got up from his desk and began to pack all his belongings. While placing important documents in his briefcase, he glanced at the monitor that still showed civilians entering and exiting the post office. In a presumptuous manner, he turned the footage off assuming that nothing was going to happen that would be vital to solving the case.

Xavier's cell vibrated once more and he opened the text: "It's a surprise, papi." He smiled and then double-checked his office, making sure everything was in proper condition. Xavier knew that the janitorial staff would take care of anything he missed or left out. He picked up his briefcase, turned out the lights, and walked out his office. He realized there were only several other detectives still here, along with his assistant Laura. Xavier hurried out the station, anxious to see Rosario, who indeed distracted him from focusing on his post office case. He walked to the side of the building where he parked his Camaro, reached into his left pocket, retrieved his car keys, and hit the unlock button. Xavier placed his briefcase in the back seat then closed the door. He opened the driver's side door, entered, and put the key in the ignition. His Camaro came to life and the engine revved, indicating it was ready for optimal performance. Xavier quickly texted Rosario back, stating he was on his way and told her to put something sexy on. Fortunately, for him she only lived a few blocks from the police station and his apartment complex as well. Xavier sped out of the parking lot and onto the main highway, eager to get to his destination. It literally only took him several minutes to arrive at Rosario's home. He pulled in her driveway, quickly parked, and pulled the keys out of ignition. He unfastened his firearm holster and placed it on the passenger's seat. Even though he hadn't changed or freshened up, he still looked presentable since he wore casual clothes today. Xavier pulled the trunk lever, exited his vehicle, and grabbed a silky black jacket that complimented his casual outfit.

"Always be prepared for situations just like this," he said to himself. Xavier checked the inside left pocket of his jacket and pulled out two Magnum XL condoms and then placed them back inside his pocket. He secured and locked his Camaro, pressing the lock button on his car keys, walked toward Rosario's front door, and knocked twice. Xavier waited patiently for the door to open. Seconds went by and Xavier attempted to knock again but halted because his cell phone vibrated.

He touched the incoming message icon and read Rosario's text, which plainly stated: "Doors open." Xavier turned the doorknob and entered the home of Rosario Esperanza and closed the door behind him. He stood on the welcome mat and didn't budge until he was greeted properly by Rosario who looked ravishingly perfected in beauty.

"Hola, detective," said Rosario with a sexy Hispanic accent.

"Good evening, Rose," he replied smiling.

"Come in, baby," she insisted, taking off his coat and leading him to the dining room. Her house had a nice atmosphere and a sweet cinnamon aroma that filled the air. The dining room was set up exquisitely with candles lit amongst dim lights, and a full course meal prepared on her glass dinner table. Rosario pulled out a chair for Xavier. "Ready to eat, papi?" she asked. He looked Rose over and slowly could feel his penis grow into a solid rock-hard erection. She had on a skin-tight sexy red dress that revealed her thick, curvy shape. She had large firm round breasts, a voluptuous rotund booty with thick hips and thighs. She wore dark red closed-toe heels that suited her outfit nicely.

"You look lovely," Xavier complimented.

"Gracias," she replied glancing at his groin area. She noticed the bulge in the middle of his pants and smiled sexily. "Not yet, mi amor," she said motioning for him to have a seat. Xavier obeyed and was seated comfortably in front of what looked to be a well-cooked delicious meal. The two indulged in a variety of Caribbean dishes that Rosario prepared for the evening. Xavier's taste buds were extremely delighted after he devoured Spanish rice, pastas, curried goat, and oxtails. The food was delectable and Xavier was overjoyed and pleased with how satisfied he became as he leaned back in his chair and stared at the woman who sat across from him. "Are you ready for dessert, love?" Rosario asked smiling. Xavier let out a long, deep breath and paused for a moment.

"I'm full," Xavier exhaled loudly while rubbing his stomach. Rosario eased up out of her seat and removed the empty plates and wine glasses from the dinner table. She strutted her sexy, elegant body gracefully toward the kitchen. Xavier refused to blink as his eyes were fixated upon the beauteousness of Rose's outstanding, curvaceous, thick body. As soon as she entered the kitchen he rose from his seat and quickly pursued her. Xavier caught Rose preparing to wash the dishes they'd just eaten off of, and he just stared. He admired her housewife qualities and over-achieving tendencies of pleasing him whenever he visited. Xavier licked his lips as he carefully studied her. He had wanted her the moment she welcomed him inside the house, and gazing at her forced an intense erection. Rose's honey complexion seemed to radiate from the kitchen light, making her glow even more beautifully. Xavier marveled at the voluptuary sight of Rose's plump booty and the way her hips swayed while she washed dishes. He walked toward Rose and stopped directly behind her so that he could adjoin his manhood against her arse. Xavier ran his fingers through her smooth, silky brunette hair which smelled like cinnamon and cocoa butter due to Herbal Essence shampoo. He leaned close to her ear. "I missed you," Xavier whispered softly. He then sucked hard on her neck attempting to arouse her.

"Mm, papi," Rose cooed as she put down the silverware she'd finished washing. Xavier tongued down Rose's neck and breathed over her upper back which sent chills down her spine as he sucked on her sensitive spots. He slowly lifted her red dress and was overjoyed when he discovered that she wore no panties.

"You were expecting this," he breathed in her ear as he unbuckled his belt and unzipped his pants allowing them to drop to the floor. Xavier whipped out his thick, bulging nine-inch phallus and rubbed it against Rose's clit from behind. He swirled the head of his penis on Rose's moist pussy lips which stimulated and aroused her.

"Aye, papi, I want you to give it to me," she whispered back in an exotic Hispanic accent. Her words were like ecstasy to his ears and encouraged him to enter her profusely wet canal.

"Damn, you're so tight and wet." Xavier shuddered from the intense feeling of Rose's vaginal wall contracting around his thick girth. Rosario moaned loudly and gripped the kitchen counter while spreading her legs. Xavier could not process anything except how good it felt. She was so wet that he knew it would not be long before he came. "Damn Rose, this pussy good!" He thrust in and out of her hastily and felt her pussy muscles constrict around his dick each time.

"Get it, papi. Take this pussy!" she cried, pushing her sex back at him. Xavier grabbed Rose's hair and yanked her head bringing her face close to his.

"Rose! I'm gonna…ahh…goddamn!" he groaned loudly through clenched teeth as he erupted inside Rose's warm nest. After he released a long hard nut inside her he collapsed on her backside, panting. Rose allowed him to regain his composure before slowly drifting away from him. Her dress fell back into place as his flaccid penis slipped out of her juicy wet pussy.

"Vamos, papa," Rose said sexily as she led him by the hand. She had not yet had her release and was determined that they both would fall asleep adequately satisfied. Xavier clutched his pants and eagerly followed closely behind Rose to her bedroom. As soon as they entered her dark bedroom Rose flicked a switch that turned on a nightlight that made her pitch black room dim. Xavier remained oblivious to his surroundings since his attention was solely focused on Rose.

"Sit down," he commanded. She obeyed and sat on the edge of the bed and crossed her smooth legs. Xavier swiftly removed his shirt, revealing a strong, sturdy upper body with firm abs.

"Mm," Rose moaned and licked her lips as she examined Xavier's muscular body. He had been visiting the weight room more frequently and reaped tremendous results. Xavier slowly took off Rose's red heels and set them aside on the floor. He always had an obsessive foot fetish and was pleased that Rose kept her feet maintained. Xavier rubbed Rose's French-pedicured right foot which felt smooth and moisturized. Everything about her feet were flawless without a trace of dirt, germs, or any of the normal compression resulting from the shoes she wore. Xavier stared seductively at Rose as he began kissing and sucking her feet in adoration, tasting traces of cocoa butter lotion. Rose melted as Xavier slowly worked his way up to her legs sucking intensely from foot to inner thigh. "Oh sí, mi rey señor," she cried twitching uncontrollably every time he tongued a sensitive area. Xavier parted her legs and once again lifted her dress far enough to expose her slimy pink pussy. Rose smiled at the excitement she saw in his eyes. "Take it, papi, it's yours," she encouraged. Xavier obliged and began feverishly licking her clit. Rose squealed in delight as her head fell back and eyes rolled. Her womanhood smelled sweet and tasted creamy with how wet she was. His tongue explored her clitoris and anus and he sucked hard on both openings. "Oh god!!" Rose squirmed and screamed in pleasure. Xavier pinned her down to keep her from escaping. He used two fingers to massage and masturbate her clit while alternating between licking her anal and vaginal crevices. "Ooh, shit!" Rose shook violently and exploded in his mouth. Xavier smiled to himself and continued to tongue her down in a truculent manner. "Aye…stop papi…it feels too good!" she shrieked as she tried to crawl away. Xavier ignored her pleas, held her down forcefully, and licked her in circular motions while fingering her. "Ahh baby!! Damn!!" She grabbed his head and flooded his mouth again with her sweet juices. She trembled as the tingling sensation surged throughout her body.

Xavier finally set her free, allowing her to recuperate and regain her composure. He slid out of his pants and boxers and got on top of her and stared at her lovely brown eyes for a moment. "You're so gorgeous," he complimented.

"Gracias," she replied, breathing heavily. She squirmed out of her red dress with Xavier's help and exposed her sexy body. Xavier immediately palmed her large breasts, pressed the pair together and sucked on her brown, hardened nipples. He squeezed her melons and licked all around her bosom that sent shockwaves through her body. "Mm," she moaned in delight. Rose was already so heated and aroused that she reached for his cock and guided it to her warmth where it fit perfectly. She took full control of the rhythm despite being on the bottom––she rolled her thick hips in circular motions while he pumped in and out slowly.

"Damn girl," he groaned. She was maneuvering her pussy good from the bottom, and he knew she'd be better on top. In one swift motion he rolled over and switched with her so she could ride his dick. Rose started out with a slow circular motion, contracting her muscles around him, causing to bite his own bottom lip. She then accelerated with fierce alacrity into a bucking bounce. Her pussy lips began smacking from the juices dripping out of her. Rose looked down at Xavier and knew he was nearing his release. She placed his palms on her breasts and rode his dick until he shot his hot thick sperm inside of her. Exhausted, they fell asleep in each other's arms, naked.

* * *

Xavier only lived a few minutes around the corner, so he made it safely to Serenity Apartment complex and parked in a convenient space. He turned his Camaro off and removed the key out of ignition. Xavier grabbed his briefcase and gun holster that carried his Springfield .45 ACP. He slowly got out of the vehicle and attached the holster to his waist before closing the car door. Xavier pressed the lock button on his keys as he made his way to his apartment. Although it was the middle of the night and pitch black, a cool breeze accompanied the distant waning moon and small twinkling stars. Xavier resided in a decent apartment complex where a majority of tenants had a credit score and income well above average. Neighbors that surrounded Xavier were educated professionals striving to achieve top status in their careers like he was. It was not difficult to adjust or acclimate to his environment since everyone seemed to be goal-oriented and aiming for more success. Xavier finally made his way to his front beige door with a gold number seven on it and inserted his key inside the doorknob lock. He unlocked his door and entered his dark, eerie home that resembled the outside night without the moon and stars. Xavier walked and maneuvered slowly until he reached the nearest light switch and flicked on the lights. The bright lights made it clear and visible for Xavier to see in the area he was standing in. Xavier stood in his small tile-floor kitchen and placed his briefcase on the countertop.

"How was your dinner detective?" said a gruff voice in the remaining darkness. In an instant, Xavier drew his firearm out the holster that was attached to his waist. He spun around to face the intruder inside his home.

"Whoever is there, don't move!" he warned, pointing his .45 at the stranger. The intruder chuckled.

"Is this how you greet all your guest's, detective?" Xavier pulled the custom slide back on his firearm.

"If they're unwelcomed," he answered.

"Oh, I can assure you that you want me to be here. Turn the lights on and see," the intruder insisted. Without lowering his weapon Xavier motioned toward the light switch and flicked it on. Xavier stared at the stranger, an elderly man who sat comfortably on his black leather sofa in the dim light. The elder wore a jet black striped suit holding a unique-looking cane shaped like a king chess piece. Xavier still had difficulty examining the man since he sat on the living room couch several feet away from the kitchen.

"What the hell do you want?" Xavier asked in a serious tone.

"I have a proposition for you. So do you mind lowering your weapon?" Xavier remained in the same position, pointing his firearm at the target. "I'm unarmed detective and I pose no threat," the elder said reassuringly. Xavier reluctantly lowered his weapon and placed it on the counter beside him.

"What do you want?" Xavier asked again in an unpleasant manner.

"I'm here to offer an opportunity. If you choose to help me I will help you," the stranger answered.

Xavier scoffed. "That's never why people break into homes," Xavier replied.

"Actually the door was open. I assume you left it open when you were rushing to get to your prison guard shift," the old man said smiling. Xavier's face turned into a distorted frown.

"You've been following me," Xavier said flatly. He slowly retrieved his firearm from the counter and held it downward at his side.

"Are you going to kill me, detective?" The old man asked. Instead of responding, Xavier glared at the old man. "If you kill me how will you solve the post office break-in?" the man inquired with a smirk on his face. Xavier's eyes narrowed due to what the man just said.

"*How did he know about that*?" Xavier thought to himself. The old man knew he had Xavier's undivided attention now and replaced his smirk with a serious facial expression.

"Lorenzo McDaniels," the elder said in a harsh tone. "Drop all of McDaniels's charges and I will give you the man responsible for infiltrating the post office. If you solve this case, you will get the promotion you always dreamed of right?" Xavier was stunned by the old man's words.

"Who are you?" Xavier asked in a calm manner. The old man rose from the sofa using his cane for support. He staggered over to Xavier and met him face to face. The light revealed a stern militant look and a scar on the left side of his face near his eye. The man appeared intelligent, experienced, and had an aura of fearlessness. "My name is Bishop Chess. I would appreciate, Xavier, if you refer to me as Mr. Chess," he insisted.

"How do you know my name?" Xavier asked in surprise. Mr. Chess walked toward the front door.

"Drop McDaniels's charges and you can solve your case," he replied as he staggered to the door. As he departed Xavier had ample time to study the man's cane closely, which besides being shaped as a chess piece, had the board game's designs all over the frame. He recollected his thoughts and memory and finally remembered where he recognized the cane from and bolted out the door. Still wielding his firearm, Xavier scanned his apartment complex parking lot and saw Mr. Chess entering a taxi.

"Hey stop!! Don't pull off!!" Xavier's shouts remained unheard and the taxi sped off before he could get close enough. Xavier was left standing in the middle of the street in the cool breeze in the midst of the dark night in awe of what just transpired. Detective Matthews knew he had a long day ahead of him…

4
REAP WHAT YOU SOW

Roman paced back and forth in a panic. He attempted to call Joyce on several occasions but it immediately went to voicemail. He was worried and anxious about why his bride left without a word to him. He already set up a police conference call in the U.S. to assist him in locating Joyce's whereabouts. Roman was in a world of confusion and couldn't make any sense of what was happening the precise moment. *"All her stuff is here so why would she leave and not say anything?"*

A knock at the door broke the trance of thought Roman was captured in. "Yes, come in," Roman said with a hint of anger. An Italian woman and two security officers stepped inside. They were dressed in a black and white military cadet uniform. Their polished black shoes glimmered in the fluorescent hotel lights.

"Good afternoon, Mr. Jacobson," greeted the officer standing on the right side. He extended his hand to shake Roman's, however, Roman remained still and just nodded his head. "My name is Officer Simon Benavidez, and this is my assistant Emmanuel Lopez," he said as he brought his hand back to his side. "We understand you think that your wife has gone missing correct?" asked Officer Lopez.

"Yes," Roman answered.

"Well our receptionist claims she saw your wife and helped her arrange for a flight to Atlanta two days ago." Roman frowned.

"Why she head back to Atlanta so soon?" he asked rhetorically. The woman who accompanied the officers stepped forward toward Roman. She definitely had dominant Italian features to where you could just see it. The woman wore a black matching blouse and skirt uniform with professional closed-toe black heels.

"Sir, when I inquired if your wife would be leaving with you she informed me that you each would leave separately," the woman explained. "She seemed to be in a hurry," she added. Roman took a deep breath and rubbed his head in frustration.

"Sir, don't worry. We've contacted the airlines and the Atlanta Police Department so if she was there, she will be found," Officer Benavidez said reassuringly. "Now if you don't mind, our receptionist will escort you downstairs to the waiting area. We need to take a look around and see if we can find anything that might help." Roman reluctantly exited his hotel room and followed the receptionist downstairs. Refreshments awaited Roman when he stepped down the stairs to the waiting area.

"Make yourself comfortable, sir," said the receptionist.

"Excuse me, ma'am, what is your name?" Roman asked in an irritated manner.

"Celia," she answered.

"Okay, Miss Celia, start booking a flight to Atlanta please," he demanded. Celia hesitated before eventually complying.

"Right away, sir," she said. Roman took a seat in the waiting area that resembled a lobby in the U.S. He took a deep breath and leaned back into his chair. All he could do was think and contemplate about his missing wife. Roman reflected on the wedding that took place three nights prior to today. It was truly the greatest moment of his life and the possibility that his other half might be in danger made his heart ache. Even though Roman had wealth, status, multiple degrees, and dependable connections, he felt useless that he could nothing about the current situation. Feelings of desperation and fear slowly began to creep in while he worried about his bride. Roman sunk his face in his hands and prayed: "Heavenly Father, I know all things work together for the good of those that love you. I ask for protection and covering over my wife and whatever she is dealing with. A man that finds a wife finds a good thing and favor with you, Lord. I pray that this passes through and we will be reunited in a safe manner, amen!" Roman concluded. As soon as Roman finished his prayer he looked up to see the two security guards coming downstairs. Roman quickly got up from his seat and motioned toward them.

"Mr. Jacobson, follow me to my office, we need to have a talk," Officer Benavidez said in a serious tone. Roman followed closely behind the two officers to a secure office room behind the reservations desk. "Have a seat, sir," Officer Lopez said, closing the door behind them. Roman sat down in a comfy leather seat and leaned forward at full attention. "We contacted the U.S. Police Department in Atlanta and they are aware of the situation. Along with that we have your flight ready and a limo outside to drive you to the airport," Officer Benavidez continued. "Before you depart I want to ask you a few questions." Roman stared at the officers.

"I'm not a suspect am I?" Roman asked. Officer Benavidez nodded.

"How long have you known your wife?" he questioned. Roman stared at him with eyebrows raised in disbelief.

"Excuse me? How is that question going to help me find my wife?" Roman inquired angrily.

"We found a crumpled up letter and photos in the disposable bin in your hotel room," Officer Benavidez answered calmly. "Maybe you should take a look," he insisted. Officer Lopez handed Roman a wrinkled up letter and three Kodak film pictures. Roman snatched the letter and photos and reviewed them. The photos portrayed a young woman who looked to be a prostitute on a street corner. She was dressed in a black mini-skirt with sandals and a small purse. However, it was difficult to see the woman's face due to the blur of how the pictures were taken. Roman studied the photos and then frowned.

"What does this mean? I've never seen this woman in my life," he said.

"Read the letter, sir," Officer Lopez suggested.

Roman sucked his teeth and read the wrinkled letter:

Dear Joyce Jacobson,

I know everything about you and what your true motives are. Everything you have done in the dark will finally come to light. Your lies and secrets will be exposed. Your past has come back to haunt you. In seven days you must return to the church you got married in to determine your future. I warn you that failure to comply will result in deadly consequences.

Sincerely, I hope you enjoyed your honeymoon.

Roman stared at the letter as if he could not comprehend it. "What the heck is this supposed to mean?" Roman asked

incredulously. "Wait a minute, are you trying to imply that these are photos of my wife!" He made the connection. "That's why you asked me how well I knew my wife," he said in a defensive manner.

"Calm down, sir," Officer Benavidez advised. "We want to help you but we need to ask these necessary questions," he added. "We know you're a wealthy man and anybody could have made this all up in an attempt to go after your finances," Officer Benavidez explained.

"Who sent this?" Roman asked.

"The sender found some way to remain anonymous," Officer Lopez answered.

"What!" Roman exclaimed. "How can you send mail without your address information?" Roman was becoming frustrated and annoyed at the two officers. He rose from his comfortable chair. "I'm going to find my wife and ask her about all this!" he said raising his voice in a furious tone. Roman left and slammed the door behind him, leaving the two officers in the office alone, and headed toward his limo. As he was about to enter the vehicle a shout from behind halted him.

"Mr. Jacobson!" Roman turned around to face Officer Benavidez once again. "I apologize we weren't much help, but when you arrive in Atlanta a detective named Xavier Matthews can better assist you," he informed. "When we contacted the U.S. they referred us to him. He will be there when your flight lands," he added. Without a word Roman entered the limo and motioned for the door to be closed behind him, but his attempt was thwarted by the officer. "Sir, there is a possibility whoever sent that letter has been watching you for some time since they're aware of your honeymoon...be careful," he warned. Officer Benavidez moved out of Roman's way and allowed him to shut the car door,

leaving him to sit in silence and think about all that took place. Roman was exhausted from being up all day trying to contact and receive whereabouts about Joyce. He knew that it would take approximately nine hours to get to Atlanta after he got to the airport and boarded his departing flight.

Roman closed his eyes and let out a deep breath before he thought about how he first met Joyce. He was donating a large sum of money at a second chance rehabilitation center and was introduced to Joyce who volunteered for community service work. She expressed how she enjoyed helping those with addictions and destructive lifestyles by counseling and mentoring them in groups. The kindness and desire to want to help those in need was indeed very attractive to Roman. He was eager to learn more about her and what she set out to accomplish in life. Roman asked Joyce out on a few dates until their friendship evolved into a closer bond. They both agreed to take the relationship slow and remained faithful to the Word of God and respected each other so that their dreams and endeavors could be achieved. After Roman completed his last semester in theology and Christian ministry, he inherited his father's churches and multi-million-dollar company of college seminars. Roman was overjoyed when Joyce accepted his proposal under the Eiffel Tower in France. Afterwards he conducted his first sermon, explaining how blessings arrive through faithfulness, walking in love, and the act of giving. He used his experience of how he met Joyce as the prime example in his first message when he preached to an enormous crowd of five hundred and fifty thousand people. Roman and Joyce dated exactly one year before he proposed on their anniversary, which for Roman was the greatest moment of his life. *"How well do you know your wife?"* Those words coincided with Roman's current thoughts. That

question infuriated him because he felt he knew his soul mate, and Joyce was his pride and joy. Certainly there were no secrets between them and the trust and commitment they shared was unbreakable, Roman thought to himself attempting to convince himself that there was nothing hidden in his marriage, despite only knowing Joyce for about a year. Joyce had no relatives and rarely spoke about her past before working at the rehabilitation center. Joyce only expressed once that her childhood was turbulent and abusive, and eventually, when she felt more comfortable, she would open up to him about it. Roman respected her decision, but now wondered if that was a mistake. Roman now started to feel unsure about himself and his wife. The letter implied that Joyce's past would come back to haunt her, and what had occurred in his wife's past was the one thing she had not talked much about to him. "No!" Roman said aloud. "I have a great wife who is honest, faithful, and trustworthy," Roman reassured himself. "This was just a scam to get my money." Roman finally convinced himself that what he was saying was true. However, in the back of his mind, he could not avoid this thought before he drifted off to sleep. *How well did he know his wife...?*

* * *

Toya Jenkins had already arranged an appointment with the Department of Children and Families and was finally prepared to get the approval she needed to get her son. She sat in the lobby and waited anxiously for the DCF representatives to call her name. After all these years there was a possibility she could really get her son back. She reminisced about her dark past as she continued to wait. She had committed many sins and was guilty of crimes she was not proud of. Leaving her kind foster parents was her first mistake that she would later come to regret. Back then when she was seventeen, she thought that was her only option and escape route when she found out she was pregnant. Toya had been rebellious and promiscuous in her early years, but everything changed when she met Lorenzo McDaniels. He had a nasty reputation that started when he was twelve from selling marijuana and cocaine, and he established his own clique by fourteen. Lorenzo was tall, dark, and a muscular smooth talker who seduced Toya into his fast-money lifestyle. She was young and foolish, which made it easy for her to fall victim to Lorenzo's lies and deceit. By the time she came to realize his con artistry, her heart, mind, and body already belonged to him. Lorenzo persuaded her to sell her body for money, along with stealing from her clients after she sexed them to sleep. Everything she ever wanted, he gave it to her. Unfortunately, it took a while before she realized the hefty price she had to pay for it. Lorenzo organized a murder to eliminate a cartel so that he could seize control of the entire drug operation in Atlanta. Somehow there was a witness who identified Lorenzo, but by paying his lawyers and the witness a large sum of money his sentenced was reduced to five years. Toya was arrested also for not cooperating with the police and refusing to elaborate on any details that could help the investigation. She was released after thirty days, but without Lorenzo her life took an unexpected detour. Toya did not know how to survive on her own on the streets and she was a target since she had the reputation for giving up the goodies then robbing you after. She experimented with drugs left behind by Lorenzo and soon became addicted to cocaine and oxycodone. Around this time came the first indication of a possible pregnancy when she vomited after one of her frequent visits with Lorenzo. She was always nauseous and felt ill after that particular visit. The recurring sickness forced her to go to the hospital where doctors examined her and gave her the news: you're pregnant.

"Toya Jenkins!" yelled the representative at the front desk, snapping her out of her thoughts. Toya quickly rose to her feet and walked toward the front desk. "Yes ma'am," Toya replied in a nervous tone. "They're ready to see you now, good luck," said the black representative with a smile. The halls reminded Toya of the clinic to which she was admitted to help with her addictions during her pregnancy. The air-conditioned room contained blue chairs arranged in rows of six, a water fountain, and a thirty-two-inch flat screen that portrayed various health care insurance policies. Toya pushed through the tan double doors and was greeted by her former probation officer and the DCF representative that took her son. "Hello, Ms. Jenkins," they both said cheerfully.

"Hi," she responded.

"You look great," the DCF representative said awestruck.

"Thanks," Toya replied and followed the two to a small office. They each sat down.

"Well my name is Mrs. Noreen and I'm sure you remember Blake your old probation officer." The DCF representative was a dark-skinned woman with a southern accent with a gold tooth that stood out among straight white teeth. Blake was a tall, bulky, white, clean-shaven man with short black hair, and was in about his mid-thirties. Noreen looked young, probably in her late twenties, and although she appeared very educated she looked as though she could bring out her true sisterhood roots if necessary. "Okay, we reviewed your applications and saw all the progress you made thus far...congratulations!" Noreen said with excitement. "You've successfully completed the community service work at the rehabilitation center along with no further involvement in previous criminal activity," she added nodding in approval. "All the fines you have incurred have been paid off, excellent!" she said smiling warmly. Noreen closed the folder that contained Toya's application and personal records and finally asked, "Are you ready to see your son?" Toya nodded.

"Please," she said almost in a pleading manner. All three of them rose from their seats enthusiastically and walked outside of the office.

"Right this way," Noreen directed. Toya followed closely behind Noreen until she stopped at a window and pointed. Toya slowly walked up to the window, looked through, and saw a playroom with several young children who each had numbers hanging around their necks. Some of the kids were coloring at a round table in the center of the room while others played with wooden blocks, stacking them as high as they could. The remaining kids were busy making odd-looking shapes out of Play-Doh. Noreen walked up next to Toya and whispered, "He's number seven." Toya studied each of the children closely and paused when she found her lucky number seven. The young light-skinned boy stood about three feet with a nice, smooth haircut and wore an Air Jordan blue jumpsuit with matching sneakers. Toya stared at the boy teary eyed, trying not to let her emotions get the best of her.

"My son," she whispered. "That's my son." She could no longer keep her composure and burst into tears of both pain and joy. She had been through hell in her early years but she cleaned herself up for the better and now she stood at the threshold of getting the one thing she desired to live for. Noreen hugged Toya tightly, who then sobbed on her shoulder.

"It's okay, honey," Noreen reassured, rubbing Toya's back in a circular motion. Toya wiped the tears from her eyes as soon as Noreen let her go. "Okay, now pull yourself together and sign these consent forms so that we can review your blood and drug test records. Blake handed Noreen some forms and then placed them in Toya's wet hands along with a pen. Toya took a deep breath and signed the forms despite her hands shaking as if she had arthritis. She returned the signed consent forms back to Noreen. "Thank you you're free to go in and meet him. We'll be back shortly," she said enthusiastically. Toya walked slowly and hesitantly to the door and paused directly before the barrier that separated her from her son.

"Thank you, Lord for this moment," she whispered before turning the door handle and entering a surreal moment. The children were not as loud as she anticipated and apparently that was because they were occupied in their games. The young Jeremiah sat at a round table coloring a picture he'd drawn. Toya stood a few feet behind him and observed him very closely. She was afraid to approach him after all this time but she wanted nothing more than to reconnect and rekindle their relationship. Toya slowly walked over to the table. "May I sit next to you?" she asked. Jeremiah looked up at Toya with cute brown innocent eyes.

"Sure," he replied, smiling. She followed up on his offer and sat closely beside him. Toya studied the picture he colored of a dark haired ebony woman with angel-like wings.

"Whatcha coloring?" she asked in an interested manner.

"I'm drawing what I think my mommy looks like." Toya struggled to keep her emotions under control and fought to prevent tears from falling. She cleared her throat before speaking again.

"What do you think she looks like?" she asked.

"Like an angel with brown skin and black hair...I dream about her sometimes," the boy explained. Toya's emotions once again got the best of her and tears rolled down her soft brown face and fell on Jeremiah's drawing. He looked up and saw Toya weeping. "Hey, why you crying?" he asked in concern. Toya looked at the boy teary eyed.

"Jeremiah, baby, you don't have to dream about Mama anymore."

Jeremiah looked puzzled. "Why?" he asked.

"I'm your mommy," she answered bursting in tears uncontrollably. "I'm so sorry I wasn't here for you...Mommy was sick and had to get better before coming to get you. I'm sorry!" she cried. Toya expected her son to reject her after all these years so she braced herself anticipating his reaction. Jeremiah stared intensely at the crying woman before him claiming to be his mother. He slowly got up from his chair and wrapped his little arms around her neck.

"Mama?" he whispered in her ear. Surprised, Toya squeezed her son tightly, savoring their first embrace after all these years. "Do I get to go home with you?" he asked in cute small voice. Toya reluctantly let him go to face him and smiled.

"Mama's gotta finish some paperwork and you and me are going to stay together forever...I promise." Jeremiah's face lit up with excitement and he was overjoyed he was reunited with his mom and could finally be with her. Toya glanced toward the window and saw Noreen waiting patiently at the door. She turned to her son once more. "I'll be right back okay," she said smiling. Jeremiah nodded in return, indicating he understood. Toya walked out the children's playroom and was confronted with Noreen once again.

"Hope I'm not interrupting," she said in a serious tone.

"No it's fine. Is everything okay?" Toya asked. Noreen's demeanor changed from a cheerful and enthusiastic to a firm attitude.

"We need to discuss something privately," she answered and walked away to her office. Toya followed behind and entered Noreen's office where she met a blond haired woman in a doctor's uniform. The nurse closed the door behind Toya and motioned for the three to take a seat.

"Hello, Ms. Jenkins, I'm Nurse Greene. How are you doing today," she greeted politely.

"What is this all about? I just want my son," she retorted.

"That's not going to be possible," Noreen interjected. Toya raised an eyebrow.

"Excuse me?"

Noreen frowned back at Toya. "We have the test results back from the labs, and although you are negative for drugs and narcotics you tested positive for HIV," informed Nurse Greene. Toya stared in disbelief, wondering if she had heard incorrectly.

"What did you just say?" she asked in a whisper. Nurse Greene looked upon Toya sadly.

"Unfortunately ma'am, you're HIV positive."

5

SOLVING THE PUZZLE

Xavier slouched on his black silk sofa, feeling angry with himself. He could not fathom what took place the previous night. An elderly man trespassed in his home and in some way blackmailed him so that he could release a convicted felon. Mr. Chess obviously planned this accordingly because now he really had no other choice. Xavier worked diligently for years in his agency building a credible reputation and the threat of being exposed as a fraud was a risk he was not willing to take. Xavier had already launched the download sequence procedure to get all background information on both Lorenzo McDaniels and Bishop Chess. He needed to piece together any relationship or specific motives they had toward one another. If Xavier could gather any useful information concerning these two men then he could utilize it against Mr. Chess and put an end to the post office case altogether. "*Download complete,*" chimed the automated female voice on his laptop. Xavier quickly moved the cursor to click on the open-file icon. Instantly a short biography timeline emerged and background information about Bishop Chess appeared on the computer screen. Xavier did not hesitate scanning the intel he received, and read aloud, "Bishop Cornelius Chess, sixty-one years of age and born on March 21, 1953 in Detroit, Michigan. Drafted to the Marines at eighteen and fought in three tours: Afghanistan, Iraq, and Korea." Xavier continued to read the articles that popped up on his laptop regarding this mysterious elder, "Former soldier is awarded the purple heart for saving his comrade and losing his right leg in the process from a land mine."

"*So that's why he walks with a cane,*" Xavier thought to himself and then retreated back to reviewing the given information.

"Former Marine champion of several chess tournaments while serving his country, parents deceased, never married, and survived by no children." Xavier clicked on a tab to carefully review any arrest records or felonies that may have been expunged and stared intently at the screen. He let out a deep breath. "Okay so you have been discharged honorably, have no criminal history, and have been retired for several years," Xavier summarized. Xavier was indeed confused but believed he might gain some answers and insight after reading McDaniels's files. He quickly typed and input the convicted felon's name and his background information immediately downloaded. Once again Xavier read the summarized biography to himself.

"Lorenzo Avery McDaniels twenty-eight years of age, born June 10, 1986 in Atlanta, Georgia. High school dropout, numerous arrests for possession, home invasion, and accessory to homicide." Xavier shook his head, displeased at what he read. "With a record

like this, you spent more time behind bars than anywhere else."
Xavier skimmed through Lorenzo's information and stopped at
his dependents. "You have a son," Xavier said surprised. "Who's
the child's mother?" he wondered. He moved his mouse and
clicked on the immediate relatives file that contained whereabouts
of the child. "Jeremiah Avery Jenkins, seven years old, was born
September 16, 2007 in Atlanta, Georgia. The child required a
blood transfusion to prevent early death, receiving the blood from
his mother Toya Evelyn Jenkins." Xavier stared at the name for a
moment. *"Hmm why does that name sound familiar?"* He typed
in the woman's name and waited shortly for her information to
upload. Her background consisted of petty theft and prostitution.
She admitted herself in a rehabilitation center to clean herself up
and successfully completed her community service there recently,
which had been required by the state of Atlanta. Toya Jenkins,
twenty-six years of age, was also born in Atlanta, Georgia, May
2, 1988. She was an orphan and fled from her foster parents at
fourteen and began prostitution to survive. "Lorenzo probably took
you in when he discovered you on the street," Xavier whispered
to himself. Xavier reviewed the mug shots of Toya, who for some
reason looked slightly familiar. Xavier printed out the files of
information he read about of all three of his suspects. He knew
that whatever Bishop had planned on doing with Lorenzo it may
include both his son and Toya Jenkins. He desperately needed to
find this woman and her son but he was required to first release
Lorenzo before he could conduct a proper search. Xavier quickly
freshened up and threw on some clothes and shoes before heading
out his apartment to his black Camaro. It was odd that he didn't
feel any less of himself even though he knew that what he was
going to do was wrong. Xavier entered his vehicle and sped down

to the precinct where personal files were kept after the judge and jury made their decisions. He knew exactly where to look since he was aware of the crime Lorenzo was charged with and what needed to be done so that he could be freed. Xavier pulled up to the back of the police station, quickly exited his vehicle, and rushed to the back door of the building. He entered a personal office undetected where only authorized personnel could access, which he was not. Xavier quickly searched thoroughly through file cabinets until he found documents that contained Lorenzo's arrest records and conclusive evidence that was used to charge him for his crime. Lorenzo had already served a majority of his five-year sentence after he pled guilty for being an accomplice to murder. However, there were no witnesses present to corroborate the story and prove Lorenzo was actually present during the homicide. Xavier took the important documents that were used to convict Lorenzo so that nobody would be able to access the records permanently. Xavier would have to later e-mail the judge, lawyers, and district attorneys involved in the trial for Lorenzo's case to explain that all charges needed to be dropped immediately due to negligence. He would also need to elaborate on false details and state that Lorenzo was framed by the true accomplice who was still at large. Xavier quietly left the dark office unnoticed. "Hope you enjoy your freedom Lorenzo," Xavier whispered to himself. Despite being in the wrong for this Xavier actually felt relieved, especially knowing that Lorenzo would most likely end up back in prison. Xavier reveled in the fact that he was closer to his promotion since he was keeping his end of the deal. He remained undetected and swiftly made it to his office quietly without notice. He flicked on the lights and as he sat down there was a knock at the door. "Come in!"

Laura walked in and handed him a folder. "You have another assignment and it's a pretty big one," she said. "Your task is to find Mr. Roman Jacobson's wife who went missing during their honeymoon," she explained. "He'll be arriving at the Atlanta International Airport shortly where you must meet him," she added. Lorraine turned and walked out the door. "Good luck." Xavier knew whenever Lorraine was this straightforward it indicated that she stuck her neck out for him so that he could get this case and he better not let her down. Xavier was pleased that he was now assigned to two cases, and solving them both would solidify his career and upcoming promotion. He quickly strutted out his small office toward the back exit and made his way to his black Camaro so that he could proceed to the interstate. Although he was excited and eager about his about his new case he wondered why Rose had not contacted him yet. It was quite odd that he had not heard from her ever since the candlelight dinner and sexual escapade.

Xavier dialed her number on his blackberry and waited for her to answer as she usually did. After the fifth ring Xavier hung up due to his impatience and quickly texted her: hit me up ASAP. He was slightly concerned about not being able to reach Rose, which was very uncommon to him. That woman was the love of his life. Even though he was not truly faithful to her, he would do anything for her if necessary. Rosario had always been loyal to him and surrendered her heart and body to him as if they were betrothed. She spoiled him with everything he could imagine and fantasize about, but unfortunately Xavier still had those doggish tendencies that lingered within most men. He assumed that she probably chose not to respond because he had left early that night after they sexed each other to sleep. Xavier drove up the inclined ramp leading to the American Airlines section of the airport and parked in an available parking space. He scrambled through his papers and stopped until he found a blank white sheet of paper and permanent marker. Xavier unfastened the cap on the marker and wrote the name Mr. Roman in bold black letters legibly. He hopped out the car and entered the airport and examined his surroundings and what was taking place at the moment.

Passengers filled the area and were busy trying to retrieve their luggage while others were patiently waiting to speak to flight attendants to board their plane. Xavier noticed groups of people hugging relatives and loved ones, which indicated that these people may have recently gotten off their flight. He walked and stopped somewhat in between the people that were getting their belongings and others reuniting with families, and he held up the sign with Roman's name on it. He looked around, surveying the airport, searching for a man traveling alone and looking for a person they had not met.

"You must be detective Matthews," said a deep voice from behind. Xavier spun around and faced a tall, muscular brown male.

"You must be Mr. Jacobson," Xavier replied, extending out his hand. Roman shook his hand fiercely.

"Call me Roman," he insisted. "So when do we start looking for my wife?" he asked in a serious manner. Roman was not interested in any formalities or anything that did not pertain to Joyce.

"As soon as we get to the station...right this way. My car is out front." Xavier examined Roman quickly. "Where's your luggage?" he asked.

"They'll be transported to my house," Roman answered. The two made their way outside the airport to Xavier's Camaro and entered simultaneously after the unlock button was pushed.

"The police station is not too far from here. Why don't you tell me about yourself in the meantime," Xavier suggested. Roman exhaled loudly in slight frustration.

"My father is Nelson Jacobson," he stated as Xavier turned the key in ignition.

"The millionaire?" Xavier asked in surprise. Roman nodded back in return.

"Is information about me going to help find my wife, detective?"

Xavier chuckled softly. "Look, I know you're frustrated and worried, but I can assure you it is necessary to obtain information about you and those around you." Xavier drove down the airport loop and onto the interstate. "Those details will help me pinpoint whether or not your wife is missing because of kidnapping...or because she left voluntarily," Xavier added. Roman's face looked saddened.

"Well...she did leave without saying anything," he said quietly putting his head down.

"The officers who contacted you found some pictures and a letter...they think she could have been involved in something from her past." Xavier glanced at Roman for a few seconds. "What do you think?" he asked.

"I love my wife but I don't know anything about her past...now I feel skeptical because she left without a word and I'm stuck with this letter." Roman didn't know what to think of the situation now but kept his composure and hoped for a positive outcome.

"We're almost there. Don't worry, you have my word that I'll find your wife," Xavier promised. Xavier slowly pulled beside a curb near the Atlanta Police Department parking lot. "Let's head to my office," Xavier insisted as they both stepped out the vehicle.

The two men walked toward the rear side of the building with Xavier leading and entered through a back passage. Xavier knew he could bypass the other officers and all the commotion that occurred by taking this route from the back of the building. His office was closer and easier to access, so as soon as he reached it he quickly unlocked it and walked through with Roman following closely behind. "Have a seat...make yourself comfortable." Roman sat directly across Xavier's desk immediately after the lights were flicked on. Xavier did not want to waste any time with this investigation and just as he attempted to bombard Roman with a series of questions, Roman handed him a wrinkled piece of paper and some pictures.

"These are the items the officers found correct?" Xavier asked taking the items from Roman who nodded in return. Xavier leaned back into his chair and read the letter carefully and then looked up at Roman. "What do you think of this?" he implored.

"I honestly don't know, detective. She left without a word," Roman replied.

"Well you're a very successful, wealthy black man. It's possible whoever sent this used your wife as bait to get to your finances," Xavier suggested. "She could have left out of fear...maybe that is why she didn't inform you," he added. Xavier's theories calmed Roman down and changed him from thinking negatively, as if his wife had left him. Detective Matthews made a clear point of why Joyce disappeared and wasn't making assumptions like the other officers had. Xavier then examined the pictures for a long time, studying them very carefully.

"She doesn't look familiar to me," Roman said. Xavier's eyes widened and eyebrows rose as if he had seen an anomaly in the photo. "What's wrong?" Roman asked seeing the horror on Detective Matthews face.

"What d-d-did you say your wife's name was again?" Xavier stammered.

"Joyce Jacobson," Roman answered, puzzled. Xavier stared at Roman with a strange look.

"When did you two meet?" he interrogated.

"Um, a year ago...been together for a year." Xavier seemed to be preoccupied in deep thought like he was trying to figure something out that was very complex. "Is there something wrong, detective?" Roman asked his voice raising. Xavier snapped back to reality.

"Uh, yes, sorry about that," he apologized glancing at the clock on his office wall. Xavier stood up quickly and walked around his desk toward Roman in a strange manner, "Mr. Jacobson, I assure you I will locate your wife... but unfortunately, as of now, something has come to my attention," he said.

"What?" Roman asked incredulously and was bewildered by Detective Matthews words. Seeing the confusion in Roman's eyes Xavier held up his hand in a reassuring gesture.

"Sir you have to trust me. I have some things I need to take care of in order to find your wife." Xavier opened the door for Roman. "I know waiting is not easy but please be patient for about an hour. I will contact you thereafter," he continued. "Tell Laura at the front desk that detective Matthews said to give you a ride home...leave your contact info with her please," he instructed. Roman stared at Xavier dumbfounded at what he was hearing and how he strange he was acting all of a sudden.

"You better find my wife!" Roman said angrily, almost in a threatening manner. He stormed out the door and Xavier quickly shut it behind him then walked back to his desk.

Xavier pulled out a black tablet from his desk drawer and typed in some information hastily. He reviewed the photos and the tablet periodically as if he were trying to confirm the identity of the person. He placed the photos closely next to the tablet and winced at the sight. "oh no," he whispered to himself. "It can't be..."

6

MISSING ROSE

Rose's vision returned slowly, adjusting to the gloomy darkness that surrounded her as she finally became conscious. Unaware of where she was, she realized instantly that she was sitting down, but was incapable of any movement. Rose felt immensely weak and wondered if her feeble efforts in trying to move were due to temporary paralysis. Her body and clothes were soaking wet from sweating out of dehydration and her dry throat felt as if it had gone through a drought. "*Where am I?*" she thought to herself. Head throbbing, Rose inhaled deeply then gagged immediately after. The atmosphere was filled with the scents of bleach, ammonia, and gasoline. She dropped her head down to avoid the strong odors and heard a metallic object rattle against something. Rose leaned forward and tried to sit upright but her attempt was thwarted and she was unable to. She had also been denied the ability to move her arms and legs freely without restriction. It finally dawned on her that paralysis was not the cause that kept her immobile--she was either chained or strapped to the chair. At once Rose became frightened and filled with dread, she panicked while her thoughts ran wild. She yanked and pulled at the restraints that bound her to the chair.

"I wouldn't do that if I were you," growled a voice in the darkness. The snarly voice startled Rose and made her jump out of surprise.

"Who's there?" she shrieked. Rose began to horripilate, and became consumed with fear trying to grasp that she was in an unknown place, blinded to her surroundings, restricted to a chair, with a stranger amidst the darkness. A dim light was suddenly turned on and this gave Rose some clarity of where she was. She appeared to be in some sort of abandoned cellar that could be beneath a library or a church. Rose looked around to examine the room she was confined in. The brown, dusty wooden floor looked unstable, while cobwebs and spiders inhabited every corner of the cracked ceiling walls. Broken antique pictures hung on the surfaces that remained intact, alongside bookshelves and ancient furniture that occupied the small eerie space. Of course, what stood out the most was Mr. Chess, the bald elderly man who stood a few feet away, holding a cane for support. He wore a black tuxedo, a crimson red tie, polished leather suede shoes, and smiled maliciously at as he stared intently at Rose. She had not recognized this man and didn't hesitate to ask the most obvious question.

"Who are you...what do you want from me?" she asked. His intentions were unclear to her and she could not help but to sob out of fright especially from the way he smiled at her. Without a word, Mr. Chess staggered past Rose and rolled a large antique mirror directly in front of her. "Oh my god," she whimpered. She was petrified at the image of herself that was presented before her. Tears streamed down her Hispanic honey-complexion face. "Why are you doing this?" she asked wailing. Mr. Chess exchanged the smile on his face with a serious look.

"Are you a God-fearing woman, ma'am?" he asked, answering her question with a question. Rose looked upon him teary eyed and confused, unable to respond out of fear but nodded her head yes as a reply. "That's interesting." Mr. Chess moved slightly closer to Rose, who was trussed up securely to his chair. "To answer your previous questions, you are here on behalf of five other individuals who will be joining you shortly," Mr. Chess explained. "You are a vital piece of my experiment and I am eager to see the outcome of the trial. Rose's face looked puffy and red as a result of her consistent sobbing, and she still couldn't make complete sense of what he meant.

"You're not going to kill me, are you?" she whimpered. "Why am I chained up?" Her voice was now hoarse and extremely dry, and she could only speak in a volume a little over a whisper. Mr. Chess remained in the same spot staring at Rose's swollen red face.

"Your fate depends entirely upon you and everyone else involved in my experiment," he answered. "For now, the reason you are bound to that chair is so that you don't escape, obviously," he added. Mr. Chess noticed the look of confusion on his victim's face and began to elaborate. "I have been in the military my entire life," he said as he staggered back and forth pacing. "I am a man of honor, commitment, integrity, respect, and diligence." Mr. Chess paused for a brief moment and glanced at Rose. "I've never been a religious man...but if there is a God, I would sure like to find out." A wicked, malicious grin flashed across Mr. Chess's slightly wrinkled face. "Christianity is the most popular religion today, and I am determined to see whether it is false and fraudulent...or if is it the truth that is mentioned throughout the gospel," he continued. He gave her a cold, menacing stare even though the smile had not yet vanished. "You agreed earlier that you were a God-fearing woman. Were you referring to the God mentioned in this book?" he inquired reaching into his suit and pulling out a small Good News Bible.

Rose slowly nodded and whispered, "Yes." Mr. Chess limped past Rose to an area behind her, which made her heartbeat faster since she was unaware of what he was doing. She could hear what sounded like tools and metal objects banging against each other as if he were looking for a specific item. The rummaging abruptly stopped and Rose knew the man drew closer by the thumping sounds of his cane.

"Very well, ma'am," he whispered in her ear causing her to jump out of surprise. "It's time to start my trials," he announced attaching a metal skullcap-shaped electrode on her head.

"What are you doing?!" she asked, yelling frantically.

"You are a pawn on the chessboard sweetheart... Everything that happens now depends on your choices as well as the others," he said.

"What are you talking about?! What others?!" Rose yanked and tugged at the chains as she hyperventilated. Mr. Chess staggered back behind her once again and turned on an electric machine that sounded like an engine running. Rose tried to look to her sides using her peripheral vision to see as much as she could of what was behind her. By the time she stared back in front of her, Mr.

Chess stood directly in her eyesight. Her eyes bulged out. "How did you..." Rose couldn't make any sense of the scenario she was a part of. The creepy basement cellar, the eerie darkness, and the chair she was chained to with a metal helmet on her head filled her with nothing but despair. The most frightening was the man that now stood in front of her glaring at her relentlessly with piercing hateful eyes. He seemed unpredictable, and even though he explained himself a bit, she felt whatever was going to transpire would be severe and merciless.

"You claim to be a follower of Christ yet your actions are contrary to what He expresses in His book," he said. "Romans chapter eight verse seven states a person becomes an enemy of God when controlled by your human nature," he restated. Mr. Chess looked at Rose with disgust, "For years you participated in acts of sexual immorality with your partner Detective Xavier Matthews." He paused to once again examine Rose's facial expression as she let out an incredulous gasp and was taken aback by his statement.

"H-how do you know?" Rose stumbled upon her words as she finished her sentence.

"The sin that you're guilty of affects your body, which is the temple of the Holy Spirit," Mr. Chess quoted. "According to First Corinthians you physically become one with Detective Matthews, which is why it is up to your other half to rescue you." Mr. Chess smiled maliciously once again. "If he doesn't then the generator will go off and transmit two thousand volts of electricity throughout your entire body." Rose gasped at his words. "Your body will shake violently and you may dislocate or fracture some bones," he continued talking smoothly. "There will be a great possibility that you will urinate and defecate while you vomit large quantities of blood," he explained. Rose looked and felt petrified while listening to the detailed, thorough explanation of what could happen to her. Mr. Chess seemed to be enjoying the facial expression and reactions he received from his helpless victim as he described the final procedure of her possible death. "Your skin will deteriorate then melt as temperature rises, and the scent of burning flesh will permeate throughout this basement," Mr. Chess said chuckling as he turned toward a brown door that appeared to be the basement exit which she had not noticed before. Rose's face was streaming with tears.

"Please...don't do this," she begged and pleaded.

"I told you already, your fate depends upon your choices and theirs...if he loves you he will come for you," Mr. Chess said. He opened the door and paused. "Don't be surprised if you do die... because the wages of sin is death," he concluded. Mr. Chess then shut off the lights and slammed the door, leaving Rose in complete darkness to scream for help at the top of her lungs.

7

RELEASED

Lorenzo McDaniels was shocked and still in awe that he had been set free early from his incarceration. While in the taxi he kept taking deep breaths periodically, savoring the aroma of fresh air. He had already given the taxi driver the address and directions to his safe house. Before he was arrested and most of his assets were seized, he transferred a small portion of his drugs and money to the location he was heading to. Lorenzo had enough to get back on his feet immediately and re-up. However, this was only his second plan to ensure his financial stability if his first idea had not worked. Lorenzo had put his baby mama's sexy looks and thick curvaceous body to work while climbing the ladder to cartel status. He became aware of Toya's skills and potential when she began matching the amount of money he made from the clients she was sexing. While in prison he advised her to clean herself up, and get a job or do community service. He promised her that by doing this it would look good to the public and on her records so that she could eventually get their son back. Lorenzo's reasons and true intentions were far from what he promised her. He knew that Toya had a natural ability to lure and attract any man, which she perfected while she was with Lorenzo. Fortunately, Atlanta was filled with successful, educated African Americans who were wealthy and owned businesses, corporations, and world-wide companies. Lorenzo knew that a lot of blacks gave back to charities and low-income poverty-stricken neighborhoods where they were raised. Knowledge about this forced Lorenzo to rely on Toya and hope that one of these upper-class black men would notice her. Lorenzo instructed Toya to change her appearance, her attire, how she spoke, and conducted herself. He reiterated that she remain off drugs, and present herself at locations where wealthy men gathered. Lorenzo smiled to himself thinking how everything worked out perfectly in his favor and that he would have access to more money and connections. Instead of dealing with small clientele, Toya redirected her work to pursuing the men Lorenzo had mentioned. Eventually she managed to cuff a young black entrepreneur who was heir to his father's illustrious company. The taxi driver approached Lorenzo's destination, which was a pleasant-looking duplex in a decent complex called Serenity Apartments. He handed the driver a fifty-dollar bill that was initially going toward his canteen in prison. Fortunately, since he was released early he used it so that he could travel to his safe house. He exited the cab without a word and jogged toward his duplex and sprinted up the third floor. Lorenzo quickly ran up the stairs until he reached a tan door with the number thirty-six on it. A brown welcome mat lay flat directly before him, and he reached down, picked up the mat, and retrieved a silver key. Lorenzo placed the mat back down and inserted the key in the silver doorknob to enter his temporary apartment home. It was in the exact same condition when he was arrested and sent to prison. The only person who was aware of this place was his baby mama, Toya, and she could only visit in case of emergency or a desperate situation. Lorenzo walked inside the kitchen, opened the cupboard and pulled out a glass bottle of vodka and placed it on the white counter top. He opened his refrigerator and retrieved a can of sprite flicked the top open and poured the sizzling soda in the glass. Lorenzo unscrewed the vodka cap and added some into the glass filled with sprite, mixing the two together. He felt the need for a drink since he been gone so long and decided to celebrate his freedom alone. Lorenzo chased down the mixed concoction of vodka and sprite then set the empty glass back on the counter top. He savored his first real drink in about five years as he walked out the kitchen toward his black sofa and pushed it slightly to the right. Behind the sofa was an interior house vent that had no screws in place, allowing Lorenzo to pull it right off. "What the f..." He peered into the dark ventilation shaft that was completely empty with the exception of a cell phone and an envelope. Lorenzo snatched the envelope and ripped the seal to shreds to retrieve a folded letter which read:

Dear Lorenzo McDaniels,

First, I would like to say welcome home! I assume right now you're upset and wondering where your illegal assets have gone. The location of all your belongings is encrypted inside the cell phone. You must come to this location tomorrow night at 11pm if you want them back. Otherwise, the money and drugs I seized will be used as conclusive evidence to put you back in prison. This cellular device is also a GPS tracker allowing me to monitor all your movements in case you try deviating from my instructions.

Sincerely, looking forward to meeting you.

Lorenzo ripped the letter from the anonymous stranger to shreds out of anger. Throughout the years of being in the trap game he made many enemies who relentlessly tried to bring him down. It was survival of the fittest and he was a hood, grimy niggah who was built for this lifestyle. He examined the cell phone, which indeed did look like an advanced piece of technology that really could have him under surveillance. Lorenzo did not want to risk doing something foolish that could jeopardize him losing his drugs and money or cause him to be sent back to prison. He knew he had to find his baby mama immediately...

* * *

Toya wept bitterly before her reflection in front of the bathroom mirror. The shocking, horrific news that she contracted HIV had broken her spirit. She had done everything necessary in an attempt to get back the one thing she loved most in the world. Toya was on the brink of finally going home with her son but once again her choices and influences from her baby daddy put a stop to it. "Ugh, I hate him!" she cried. She had been loyal to Lorenzo and given everything to him, and in return he transferred his deadly disease to her. She heard someone enter the restroom and without a word she found herself in a tight, soothing, reassuring embrace.

"Ms. Jenkins, I know this is unfortunate news, and that more than anything you want your son back," Ms. Noreen said as she let Toya go. "The programs that we offer can help assist you in living and coping with the virus," she informed. Noreen took some Kleenex tissues from nearby and handed them to the teary-eyed, weeping Toya. "I do have some good news...there is a way for you to have a close relationship with Jeremiah." These words were the only comfort Toya heard that put a band-aid on her now knowing she was diagnosed with HIV.

"How?" Toya asked in a quiet whisper.

"There is a man who has been interested in adopting Jeremiah for quite some time and has signed partial documents to claim him," Noreen explained. "I know all this is a lot right now, but we will help you every step of the way," she added. "Take a deep breath, try to gather your thoughts...the man is in the room to the right as soon as you leave the restroom." Noreen gently touched Toya on the shoulder and smiled before she departed, leaving Toya alone in the restroom.

Toya took a deep breath and swallowed hard. She forced all the negative news she heard to the back of her mind. Toya's promise to Jeremiah that she would finally be able to take him motivated her. She wanted her son desperately, more than anything, and even though she was now paying the price for her past deeds, she vowed to pay them while raising Jeremiah. Toya exited the bathroom and followed Noreen's directions, which led to a small, secluded, vacant room, and slowly opened the door. It was a small vacant room, probably where quick meetings were held. The only furniture that was in the room was three chairs and a rectangular brown table. The chairs were adjacent to each other and were all empty of course, except the one in the center of the table where an elderly man sat wearing a navy blue suit with a matching tie.

"Hello, sir. My name is Toya Jenkins," she introduced herself, forcing a smile.

"Nice to finally meet you...my name is Bishop Chess," the elder replied. Toya took a seat close to Mr. Chess.

"I understand you want to adopt my son," she said flatly getting straight to the point. Mr. Chess nodded.

"That is correct."

Toya sighed. "Well sir, is there anything I can do to change your mind or get you to decide to possibly adopt another child?" she asked in a humble, pleading manner. Mr. Chess stared hard at Toya.

"Why do you want Jeremiah?" he asked in a harsh tone. Toya was stunned and taken aback by his question.

"Well, because he's my son," she answered with eyebrows narrowed. Mr. Chess glared at Toya.

"He's been your son for the last seven years. Where were you?" These words hurt Toya deeply but she knew that she had never been there at all. She retreated from his glare, looking down in defeat.

"I've made very terrible choices, sir… I'm begging for a second chance to get my son." Tears welled up in her eyes as she forced herself to look at Mr. Chess. He responded by staring at her intensely and threw her completely off guard with his next question.

"Where's your wedding ring?"

Toya gasped in surprise. "Excuse me?" She looked bewildered. Mr. Chess looked angrily at her with pure contempt.

"You don't recognize me do you?" he asked. Toya looked at the elder flabbergasted.

"Uh no sir you don't look familiar."

Mr. Chess repositioned himself in his chair and leaned forward, frowning at Toya. "I saw you several days ago at North Central Church of God in Christ," he reminded her. He noticed that this statement made Toya become rigid and break into a nervous cold sweat. "I was present when you became Mrs. Joyce Jacobson," he said with a smirk. That sentence made Toya cringe out of fear. This stranger somehow knew her identity and she was unaware of who he was and what he planned on doing with the information.

"W-w-what does that have to do with my son?" she asked stuttering.

"It has everything to do with your son, Mrs. Jacobson," he responded sharply. "I wrote that everything you've done in the dark will come to the light," he added with a grin. Toya's eyes widened out of shock.

"So it was you who wrote me!" she exclaimed.

"Indeed it was," Mr. Chess replied nodding. This was surreal to her and she had difficulty trying to fathom all of this.

"So you know about my past and identity... What do you want from me now?" she demanded. Mr. Chess flashed a wicked, malicious grin across his face that he was accustomed to making.

"You have your instructions from the letter, and you must arrive at eleven o'clock tomorrow night." Toya was speechless and was unable to make eye contact with the elder before her. "I have no desire to keep your son, Mrs. Jacobson...this is your second chance you've always wanted to get him back." Mr. Chess rose from his seat and grabbed his cane on the floor and staggered to the door. "I suggest you find and talk to your husband," he advised before he limped out the door.

Back at the Office

Detective Matthews was on the border of figuring out everything that had transpired. Somehow Roman, Toya, and Lorenzo were all connected in whatever agenda Mr. Chess had planned. The post office case was a tool he used as an advantage to lure a young, black ambitious detective into a form of wager. By releasing Lorenzo, detective Matthews would gain his lifetime dream and promotion as Mr. Chess had promised. Xavier had already held up his side of the deal so now all he had to do was wait patiently. It was far too late to retreat now since he had already broken the same laws he'd sworn to enforce and abide by. He sat in front of his laptop in his office and reviewed personal data about Lorenzo, Roman, and Toya. He noticed that while

Lorenzo was incarcerated Toya was not involved in any criminal activity. Instead, she'd gotten rehabilitated and freed herself from the addiction she struggled with. Roman Jacobson donated large amounts of money to rehab centers, clinics, and other various charity organizations. He was well known to the world of Christianity because of his father, a worldwide spokesperson, best-selling author, and bishop in ministry. Xavier thoroughly looked over mug shots and images of LaToya Jenkins. He had to be one hundred percent sure he knew exactly who this woman was. "Toya Jenkins *is* Joyce Jacobson," he stated whispering to himself. Apparently, she met Roman after she cleaned herself up and Lorenzo was locked up. This further explained why she left Roman after the honeymoon. Xavier now recognized her as the last woman he checked in for visitation on his shift at the penitentiary. Joyce had not gone missing after all but left to visit her son's father. What bothered Xavier was that he didn't know what Mr. Chess truly intended to do with this particular love triangle. *Beep, beep.* Xavier's cell phone alerted him, letting him know that an incoming e-mail had successfully arrived. Instead of checking his phone he signed into his e-mail account on his laptop. He navigated through his junk mail deleting old messages that were now irrelevant. He clicked on one of the unread messages that transferred him to a video media player. The buffering video loaded a dark, pitch black screen until lights were turned on. The video clip was in high definition making it very clear to see a Hispanic woman chained to an electric chair wailing, "Help!!" Xavier knew immediately who the woman was and jumped out of his chair. "Rose!" His chair tipped over backwards while Xavier leaned in closely to the computer screen. The video clip ended abruptly after showing that horrific hopeless scene. Xavier quickly used the mouse to exit out of this current message to review the second. This e-mail read:

Good evening, detective

I'm sure by now you've figured out a great deal about everything. I want to thank you for helping me with McDaniels, and this message is me keeping my end of the deal. I told you I would give you the one responsible for the post office infiltration and you are probably aware that it was I. At the moment I am at the North Central Church of God in Christ waiting for you and all other participants who will arrive at 11pm. You must come along if you want a chance to apprehend me and rescue your beloved Rose.

Sincerely, Bishop Chess

Infuriated, Xavier slammed his laptop down shut and grabbed his firearm holster and attached it to his waist. He was now a victim in the love triangle that had interfered with Roman's marriage.

8

THE GAME BEGINS

Even though she was in the midst of a horrific torture chamber in a basement cellar Rose somehow now managed to remain calm. She felt at ease believing her knight in shining armor was coming to her rescue. Aside from that belief, she felt as though she were nothing more than a pawn to lure in Mr. Chess's true victims. He had not inflicted any physical harm to her while she was confined to the electric chair. Whenever he spoke or answered her questions, it was in a polite manner with respect, despite his gruff tone of voice. Rose had difficulty understanding what all this was really about even though the elder explained in detail why she was involved. There had to be a deeper more sinister scheme he planned on carrying out. Mr. Chess mentioned that the outcome of everything was solely dependent upon the choices of each individual. Rose's intuition led her to think that all who were involved in this demented fantasy probably had something to do with Xavier. He was a detective for Christ sake, maybe her kidnapper had an issue with him and this was his way of payback.

"You seem very preoccupied in thought," Mr. Chess said in a raspy voice. He sat several feet away from Rose's electric chair behind a desk area with computers.

"You know when Xavier finds me he's going to kill you," Rose said confidently. Rose was no longer intimidated or afraid of him.

"What makes you so sure?" Mr. Chess asked curiously.

"He loves me," she answered with her strong Spanish accent.

"Hmm." Mr. Chess paused and thought for a moment. As he was about to speak, his focus reverted back to the computer screen. "Ah, well I guess we're certainly about to find out," Mr. Chess said. He rose from his desk and staggered out the basement cellar leaving Rose behind. Mr. Chess made his way to another upstairs room, which looked to be a control room with various updated technology. He watched a television monitor of live security camera footage of LaToya, Lorenzo, and Xavier outside the church. They each looked angry and confused and began noticeably arguing with each other. Toya was dressed in all-black, matching outfit with Jamison riding boots, which she probably wore in an attempt to conceal her identity and remain secretive. Lorenzo wore black Timberlands, black jeans, and a gray long sleeve shirt. Xavier, however, naturally wore his crime scene investigation attire with his usual firearm holster. Mr. Chess watched the live feed closely and noticed that Xavier kept his composure and eventually calmed Toya and Lorenzo down. The animosity between the two could easily be seen as if they had a long history of rivalry. Mr. Chess was unable to hear audibly what was being said since they were currently outside and he had set up his equipment inside the church. He had done that so the lines would remain secure and no outsider could hack into the security footage and hear anything. The trio seemed hesitant about entering the church until detective

Matthews made the first move toward the door. Xavier was taking no chances and grabbed his firearm from his holster and brought his ear to the door to listen to any sounds within the church. Lorenzo was apparently armed as well and followed closely behind Xavier with Toya reluctantly walking alongside him. The two men obviously had come to common ground when they whispered something to each other and kicked the church doors open.

"*Let's get started,*" Mr. Chess thought to himself. As soon as the three entered the sanctuary hall they stopped abruptly. Dim lights immediately turned on and all over the walls were signs and directions telling each of them where they should go. While each of them surveyed the church, a microphone intercom transmitter was turned on, allowing each of them to hear Mr. Chess.

"Good evening participants and welcome!" he said warmly. "I appreciate that you all remained punctual and arrived on time. Finally, we may begin!" he said enthusiastically. "You are all here because I have something that you want dearly...whether or not you to get them back will depend entirely upon you," he explained. "There are hints and clues that I suggest you use as guidelines to help you through. Each of your decisions will determine the outcome of tonight. Good luck." Mr. Chess sat back in his chair in the control room and watched the monitor screen closely. He knew that they did not want to separate but detective Matthews would be making decisions for them if they stuck together. Mr. Chess increased the volume so he could hear what they were saying.

"We all have to go our separate ways," detective Matthews said. He stared at the rose-petal trail toward the right of the church. He knew exactly what Mr. Chess was insinuating and was determined to find the woman he loved. Xavier turned to face Toya and Lorenzo. "Look, I don't know what personal agendas you guys have, but the instructions were very clear," he said. "Use the hints and clues before making your decisions," he reiterated. Xavier walked toward Toya and handed her a smaller firearm he kept strapped to his leg under his jeans. "Here... I trust you know how to use this...I've seen your record." Xavier quickly motioned toward the trail of red rose petals eager to find his beloved. Toya and Lorenzo watched as Xavier departed then stared at each other. Toya glared at Lorenzo with a whirlwind of mixed feelings. Anger, disgust, hurt, hate, and disbelief swept over her like a hovering cloud. She squeezed the gun in her hand tightly, debating on whether or not she should kill him. He was the reason for the good, bad, and ugly in her life. How could she be upset though when Lorenzo had explained his lifestyle to her and she knew very well how the game went and how it was in the street. Money was always the main objective and they both hunted it down no matter what the cost. They each paid a hefty price and were guilty of faithlessness and infidelity. Despite all this, she still had strong feelings for him that would never be erased.

"Make sure we get our son back!" Toya said in a harsh tone of voice and walked away. She saw two arrows pointing to a side exit toward the left. The arrows contained messages which read: twenty-fourth book of the Old Testament and prophet to the nations. Toya searched the pews near her and found a Bible already opened on the table of contents page. She counted the books of the Old Testament until she reached twenty-four. The twenty-fourth, coincidentally, was Jeremiah. Immediately Toya dropped the Holy Bible and fled toward the exit where the arrows had pointed. Lorenzo witnessed all this occur but remained motionless. Lorenzo's directions led him to the pulpit where his name was projected on an overhead screen. He made his way to the pulpit which had a sheet of paper that read: *I want you to sit and read Romans and First Corinthians thoroughly! After that, you will wake up to your next objective.*

Lorenzo exhaled loudly in a frustrated, aggravated demeanor. He knew he had to follow through with this to get his money and drugs, and to avoid prison time. He looked around until he found a Bible and sat down on a pew beside it. Lorenzo searched and eventually found Romans and began reading carefully. He rarely ever read the Bible and dreaded those times he was asked to do so in prison, since it was difficult to comprehend. However, this particular version of the Bible Lorenzo was instructed to read was in modern day English. Lorenzo slowly began reading Romans word-by-word and chapter-by-chapter. The scripture suggested how the Gospel revealed that God put us right with Him through faith. After the fall of Adam, mankind had been plagued with sin until Christ gave His life, which proved to be the ultimate sacrifice. Pleading for forgiveness and beginning a new life in union with Christ Jesus freed anybody from sin and the second death. It was mentioned how a believer should live his life demonstrating the agape love of Christ. Examples, illustrations, and descriptive details were shown well enough for Lorenzo to fully grasp what he was reading. He noticed that no matter who you were and what sin you'd committed, salvation would be accessible to everyone. Lorenzo paused for a moment reminiscing on all the wrong he had done in his life. He participated in various armed robberies, shootouts, drug trafficking, and even pimped his baby momma! In the streets everybody knew that love and mercy were considered weaknesses, so how could the Lord be merciful enough to forgive him? It was all surreal to him that the salvation that all the preachers spoke about was this *simple*. In prison, Lorenzo refused to listen or pay close attention to the chaplain because he thought Christians were judgmental and lived by all these complicated rules. Now for the first time it was summarized to him stating that we are all sinners that needed Jesus--not that everyone should be perfect and point fingers at others. In spite of all the passages he read so far Lorenzo was not convinced that he could be forgiven. He flipped the page to the next chapter of First Corinthians and proceeded in reading. This portion of the Bible was vastly different from Romans and elaborated on topics that most people questioned. Lorenzo was in an era of immorality, homosexuality, gender transitions, woman exploitation, and degradation. Some of these were justifiable by the Constitution's freedom, rights, and fairness laws. This was discussed in the chapters Lorenzo read thoroughly and carefully. The first question that ran across Lorenzo's mind was immediately answered where he read about the divisions in the church. He always wondered growing up why there were so many different churches that claimed to believe in the same God. The scripture explained how all should be united with one thought and purpose as servants of Christ. Overall, what stood out the most to Lorenzo were the topics on sexual immorality, fornication, adultery, marriage, and the greatest commandment, *love.* The chapter described how to treat your wife in marriage, and to remain abstinent, pertaining to those without a spouse. The scripture was very specific in detail when explaining the severity of premarital sex. Whenever you have intercourse with a person you become one with your mate and a bond between your souls is forged. In God's eyes marriage and the body referred to as the temple were sacred and taken very seriously. Lorenzo was guilty of not abiding by this and for some odd reason he felt a sense of conviction. He had been harsh and cruel to Toya for the majority of their relationship. The sweet, loving, innocent girl he'd first met when they were teenagers was now cold and heartless. Lorenzo molded her this way to be ruthless and have a mindset of a hustler so making money would be her main priority by any means necessary. In the passages that Lorenzo read it informed him that the man was positioned to be the head of the household requiring him to lead his family in the right direction. Lorenzo certainly did lead Toya, however, it was down a path of destruction and ruin. As he continued to read he felt the strong overwhelming feelings of guilt and sorrow. For the first time in his life, he regretted the things he had done and strangely felt the urge to repent. As he sat in the wooden pew in a large church reading the word for himself a change of heart seemed to miraculously be taking place. After reading the chapters and verses he was requested to read all he could think about was Toya. He thought of the many possibilities and different scenarios of how her life could have been better without him. Lorenzo always knew she had great potential to excel in life. From the first time he gazed upon her, she looked stunningly beautiful and had the traits of loyalty. She was the ideal choice that a man would pick for a wife before he corrupted her. Lorenzo groomed her into a manipulative, recalcitrant woman able to survive in the streets of drugs and prostitution. He now realized that was no excuse when he could have worked honestly and steered away from his current lifestyle. At the present moment, he wanted nothing more than to plead forgiveness for the sins he committed. Lorenzo finally realized he was to blame for all this and was willing to accept whatever fate was in store for him tonight.

Meanwhile

Xavier walked cautiously down a dark corridor with both his firearm and a small but bright LED flashlight. As he came near a corner he quickly waltzed around it only to be confronted with a brown wooden door with a sticky note on it. Xavier shone the light on the note and read the legible words: *Roses are red, violets are blue/ your love lies beyond this door, waiting for you.* Without a second thought, Xavier instinctively and swiftly kicked down the door. He walked into a dim lighted room and saw Rose directly in front of him. An overhead light was swinging back and forth above her head while she remained motionless in an electric chair. He quickly motioned toward her but was forced to stop abruptly by the glass barrier he failed to notice. Xavier examined the glass that stood before him and the love of his life and realized it was bulletproof.

"Damn," he cursed under his breath. Xavier stared at Rose who was unconscious and looked like she'd been through hell and back. Her head hung low and her jet black, silky hair covered her honey, caramel face. He studied her to see if there were any visible marks, scratches, or incisions of any kind on her body. No harm appeared to have been done to her but Xavier remained vigilant, knowing she was chained to an electric chair. In the midst of the dim light coming from the swinging overhead bulb above Rose, Xavier saw a silhouette of a person standing on his side of the glass. He glanced to his left to see Mr. Chess standing several feet away from him. Xavier was so focused and preoccupied on Rose he failed to notice he had not been alone. A rush of rage and adrenaline surged through Xavier's body, and without hesitation, he lunged toward the old man to attack him but his attempt was thwarted by a Taser, which stunned him immediately. Xavier dropped his firearm and flashlight as he fell to the floor shaking and twitching from the jolts of electricity. Mr. Chess limped toward the detective kneeled down and picked up his flashlight and firearm. He took the magazine out of the 1911 Colt and checked to see if there were any rounds in the chamber. Mr. Chess put the gun in a holster he had in the back of his leather suede blazer and waited patiently for Xavier to regain his composure. Slowly Xavier was able to get back to his feet and stand face to face with the man who started all this. "Shall we do this again properly," Mr. Chess suggested.

"Let her go," Xavier replied through clenched teeth, ignoring the old man's suggestion. Mr. Chess smiled in return.

"Straight to the point," he retorted, glancing at Rose. "I wonder if Moses and Aaron told the Pharaoh to let the Israelites go in the same manner you're doing now for her," he said. Xavier was puzzled and gave the elder a strange look. "My apologies...I have been reading the Bible for some time now and that is what inspired me to carry out this plan," Mr. Chess explained, staggering to the bulletproof glass. "You see, detective, I want to know for sure whether the Bible is true or false," he said revealing his intentions. "I believe after tonight I will have my answer," he said snickering. Mr. Chess turned to look at Xavier directly in his eyes. "Do you know why I left her life and the opportunity to be rescued in your hands?" Mr. Chess asked curiously.

Xavier shook his head. "No." he answered.

Mr. Chess cleared his throat. "When Jesus was arrested and brought before Pontius Pilate who was aware of his innocence, Pilate let a crowd of people choose the fate of Christ," Mr. Chess explained. "The crowd wanted an innocent man to be crucified instead of a murderer named Barabbas, who was set free," he continued. Xavier frowned upon hearing this short story of an innocent man being condemned while a guilty man was left unpunished. It was the first time he had heard this excerpt from the Bible. He'd never been a religious man. Mr. Chess could see the frustration in Xavier's eyes. "How does that make you feel detective?" he questioned.

"A little upset, but what does this have to do with Rose?" he replied with a question.

"Everything," Mr. Chess answered. "Rose is an innocent victim who has done nothing legally wrong," Mr. Chess explained. "I am the criminal like Barabbas and I am guilty of breaking into the post office, your house, and kidnapping your lovely Rose," he admitted smiling. "Since you're the detective you should be able to figure out who you are," Mr. Chess said.

"Pontius Pilate," Xavier answered.

Mr. Chess nodded. "Correct, and the outcome of all this is in your hands." Xavier looked at Rose.

"I want you to let her go!" he demanded angrily.

"Are you sure about that detective? Initially you should apprehend me for the crimes I've committed, and as planned you will have the promotion you always dreamed of," Mr. Chess reminded him. He pointed at Rose. "She deserves to go free and I deserved to be punished for my crimes…just like you do, my accomplice." Xavier's jaw tightened at the elder's words. He knew he played a role in helping Mr. Chess with his plan while knowing he was a possible suspect. Everything he worked for and dreamed of was at the tip of his fingers, depending on his decision. Xavier looked intensely at Rose who remained unconscious, confined to an electric chair, and he thought of the outcome if he rescued her. It would result in his termination and incarceration for compliance with Mr. Chess and his heinous crimes. The promises he made to

Rose of marriage and his job promotion would be broken and he would be a liar and a felon.

"If I arrest you what makes you think I can't save her?" Xavier asked glaring. Mr. Chess chuckled.

"Ms. Rose is not unconscious because she is tired, detective. It is because of the lack of oxygen she is receiving in that room," he answered.

Xavier's eyes widened. "What!?"

Mr. Chess was not sympathetic in the way he revealed the news. "The people who killed Jesus made a choice to crucify Him while the criminal went free...someone has to live and someone has to die," he explained. "Arresting only me and letting yourself go free would result in her death, detective... similar to how it was decided that Jesus, the innocent one, was sent to his death." Xavier stared at the elder with pure contempt. "If you save her you would only be giving up what you worked so diligently for all these years...your future." Xavier swallowed hard. "Love thy neighbor as you love thy self, detective," Mr. Chess quoted. Xavier looked down to the floor in deep thought. He never could've imagined ending up in a twisted situation quite like this.

"You lied to me and set me up!" Xavier shouted.

Mr. Chess calmly shook his head. "You had an opportunity to arrest me at your house and I offered you a deal where I promised to surrender myself if you complied." Xavier clenched his teeth and tightened his fists. "The decision is yours to make, detective," Mr. Chess reminded him. Xavier took a few steps until he was only a few inches from the elder's face.

"You're going to prison, and if she dies then you die," Xavier threatened.

Mr. Chess was not intimidated. "So you've decided to arrest me, correct?" Mr. Chess asked validating the decision. Xavier grabbed the elder before him and threw him to the ground effortlessly. He searched his suit and pockets thoroughly and found his magazine to his 1911 Colt and his firearm, which he retrieved, and then inserted the magazine inside his gun. As he was about to pull the slide back to chamber a round in his firearm lights flashed on the opposite side of the glass where Rose sat. The lights flashed around a small electronic box that looked like a generator or engine. Xavier could see electric currents and jolts of electricity around Rose as the generator began to vibrate violently. Rose was mildly electrocuted and the jolted impact of electricity brought her back to consciousness. Xavier ran to the bulletproof glass and banged on the window in an attempt to get her attention. It appeared that the generator somehow began to malfunction and shook rapidly with smoke arising. A spark from the generator created a small fire that would unfortunately spread throughout the room that contained Rose. She was helpless in the chair that bound her and Xavier, who was full of despair, was incapable of saving her.

"Rose!" Xavier pulled the slide back on his firearm and shot several rounds at the bulletproof glass. After the loud deafening noise of the shots fired came a banging sound from behind Xavier near the door from where he entered. He spun around quickly and noticed that Mr. Chess had quietly left. Xavier sprinted toward the door and turned the knob and to his surprise, he was locked securely in. The noise apparently had been Mr. Chess barricading the door shut. "I'll kill you old man!" Xavier shouted, banging loudly on the door with his heavy fists. Xavier was so concerned with breaking the door down he failed to notice the pain and agony

Rose was experiencing. A bloodcurdling scream finally got Xavier's undivided attention. He turned and saw the most horrific sight in his life. Rose was surrounded by a ring of fire that was closing in on her fast, and smoke inhalation would soon be making it difficult for her to breathe. Xavier was all out of options and would be forced to witness the slow, painful death of the love of his life. He checked his firearm and there was one round left within the magazine. Xavier once again looked beyond the window and watched as Rose was consumed by the fiery red-orange flames. Guilt and sorrow swept over him like a dark, hovering cloud. He was at fault and to blame for this situation and now had to watch everything he desperately wanted go up in flames. His career would be over once the truth was revealed about his cooperation with Mr. Chess and he would be deemed accomplice to murder. Silence was drowned out by the screams and cries of Rose who slowly endured one of the most painful ways to confront death because of him. He made the choice even though he knew what the consequence would be. It seemed as though guilt and grief punctured a wound his heart which he could no longer bear. Xavier raised the 1911 Colt toward his temple slowly while he saw the remaining flesh on Rose's skin turn black as coal from the scorching flames.

Awaited Arrival

Roman had no desire to wait on any officers or state authorities and deviated from Detective Matthews's instructions. As soon as the driver of the yellow-checkered taxi pulled beside the curb directly outside the church, Roman paid the exact amount due and rushed out the vehicle. Unaware of the impending danger, Roman sprinted up the church steps and barged through the antique-looking double doors. The church did not have the welcoming feel that it did when he was getting married to Joyce. Instead, the inside looked dim and gloomy and smelled like a fire had just been put out. There were signs, arrows, and words inscribed all over the sanctuary walls of the church. His concern and curiosity instinctively led him toward the direction of where the strong burning odor was coming from. Roman successfully used his senses and followed the foul odor which eventually brought him to a brown door. He paused for a moment hoping that no harm had come to Joyce. "Please be safe." Without any more second thoughts, Roman turned the knob and pushed the door open. "Oh my god!" he exclaimed. Roman's eyes widened and jaw dropped at the gruesome sight that lay before him. Detective Matthews lay on the floor a few feet away from him in a pool of blood, motionless. A large chunk was missing from the side of his head, which made his face look unidentifiable and grotesque. Roman further examined the body and noticed a firearm in Xavier's hand, indicating this was a possible suicide. Fortunately, this was not the first time Roman saw a dead body especially since he had been a pastor and preached at dozens of funerals. He continued to look around the room, and aside from the blood splattered all over the walls, he saw where the fire had taken place. The remains of a burnt corpse lay in an awkward position near what looked to be an electric chair. Roman was now petrified, unable to move, and felt extremely uncomfortable around this crime scene. He summarized and concluded that a fire started somehow and since there was no escape Xavier had shot himself while the other individual burned to death. Roman was unable to identify the corpse because of the severity of the burns, making him worry it could have been Joyce until he heard a loud scream in the distance. Hope resurfaced within Roman forcing, him to quickly exit the room toward a possibly endangered Joyce, where he would make sure she did not face a fate similar to what the two previous victims endured.

9

CHECKMATE

Toya had walked past many hallways and corridors within the church for what seemed like an eternity. She obeyed the specific directions Mr. Chess had given her which would lead to her beloved son. For his whole life, Jeremiah's estranged parents were never there for him, and Toya would rather die than to allow that to happen once more. She desperately sought out after her only child, risking everything so that he could return safely to her. At last, she finally came to a bronze door with the name Jeremiah carved into it deeply. Toya reached for the knob and whispered under her breath, "Please God, let him be okay." She slowly turned the door handle and walked inside a spacious room with a theatre-like screen that portrayed her son playing in a playroom safe and sound. Toya welled up with tears, relieved to see her son and motioned toward the screen. The room Jeremiah was sheltered in had dozens of toys such as multi-colored Play-Doh, superhero action figures, coloring books, building blocks, and a mini swing set.

"Why did you name him Jeremiah?" asked a familiar, gruff voice. Toya turned around but nobody was in sight.

"*He must be still using the intercom.*" She thought to herself. Toya let out an exasperated sigh. "I just liked the name," she replied.

Mr. Chess spoke from the intercom once again. "Jeremiah was a prophet who had one of the most difficult tasks in the bible," he informed her. "He was known as the weeping prophet who sobbed for the slaying of his own people," he added. "The prophet foresaw the upcoming destruction, chaos, and devastation, and warned the land," Mr. Chess said. Toya listened closely to the elder's history lesson knowing that he was the only who could return her son to her. "I'm going to have to ask you to be patient for a moment longer until the two men arrive." Toya assumed he was referring to Lorenzo and detective Matthews.

"What were the screaming noises and where were they coming from?" she asked.

"The repercussions of a choice that was made," he answered blatantly. Lorenzo entered the room and joined Toya who quickly got in a defensive stance folding her arms and raising her left eyebrow.

"Are you okay?" Lorenzo asked in a genuinely concerned voice.

"I'm fine," she replied through clenched teeth. Lorenzo put his head down in defeat knowing that it may be too late to apologize, let alone plead for her forgiveness. He opened his mouth to speak but was interrupted.

"I want to commend you, Mr. McDaniels, for taking the time to thoroughly read those scriptures," Mr. Chess said as if congratulating him. Lorenzo was startled by the voice from the intercom but did well to keep his composure. "I certainly do not wish to interrupt this reunion but I am eager to hear what you learned."

Lorenzo took this opportunity to not only elaborate on what he gained from those passages but to pour out his heart to his baby momma. He looked Toya directly into her angry eyes and then spoke, "I know you don't wanna hear nothing I gotta say, but please listen closely," he begged. Toya rolled her eyes and made a face.

"If you insist," she replied with a sarcastic attitude.

"I know I'm responsible for all this mess and dragged you into this lifestyle," Lorenzo began with a serious expression. "I'm a street niggah, and when I read those words from the Bible it made me stop and check myself," he continued. "I was all about makin' that money. I wasn't focusing on you and Jeremiah like I should have been, and now we paying the price," Lorenzo added. Toya remained defensive, but listened closely to his words surprised that he was actually saying all of this. "I never had a father figure, and those verses just now taught me what kind of man I'm supposed to be." Lorenzo got on both knees and wrapped his muscular arms around Toya's waist. "Please forgive me for everything!" he pleaded loudly. Toya looked down in disbelief, stunned at what she just heard and what her baby daddy just did. A tear rolled down her face as a wave of emotion came to her. In all her years with Lorenzo she never experienced him doing something like this or even seeing a sensitive side to him. To actually look down upon him pleading and begging for forgiveness with remorse and sorrow was surreal to her. However, she refused to believe him and her stubbornness came into play. Toya unfolded his arms around her waist and stepped back, quickly wiping the tear.

"Why you doing this now all of a sudden?" she asked demanding to know. "You expect me to believe a few verses changed you that fast?"

Lorenzo rose to his feet and to Toya's surprise a tear rolled down his face. "I finally see all the pain I caused you," he admitted honestly. Toya realized this was no act or facade since Lorenzo had never been one to shed tears. "I know I can't change the past or make things right, but I ask that you forgive me." Lorenzo slowly took a step toward Toya and wiped her tears. She could not resist any longer and when he hugged her tightly she melted in his arms. Despite all the pain he inflicted upon her they had a bond that could never be broken. Lorenzo leaned in closely to Toya to kiss her but his attempt was thwarted when the door behind them slammed. The noise startled Toya and her eyes grew wide when she saw who just walked in. Her husband Roman stood several feet away glaring at her with an angry and confused look on his face as he watched Toya separate from Lorenzo's embrace. Before any of them could speak the intercom broke the awkward silence.

"Glad you finally made it, Mr. Jacobson!" Mr. Chess said cheerfully. "You are the most significant piece on the board, and can drastically change the outcome of this situation," he explained. "If you all want to leave safely unharmed with what I promised to return to you then each of you must convince me of the existence of Christ," he proposed. The three of them each looked confused. "Your actions will determine what will be in store for you," he explained. "So far I have witnessed Mr. McDaniels plead for forgiveness, but will he be forgiven by his longtime lover?" he asked rhetorically. "Will Mrs. Jacobson confess her sins to her husband, a pastor who should know the importance of a second chance?" Mr. Chess cleared his throat on the intercom. "His decision ultimately will be your salvation to freedom and will definitely prove to me that the Bible and Christianity is indeed valid."

Roman stood baffled. "What the hell is going on!" he yelled angrily. Toya forced herself to make eye contact with her husband. Deep down she had love for him and never truly wanted to intentionally hurt him. "Joyce…what is going on?" he repeated. The feelings of guilt flooded her but she had to tell him the truth and pray he would forgive her. That was easier said than done when she herself had not truly forgiven Lorenzo, but she had to try for the sake of her son.

"My name is not Joyce," she said barely above a whisper.

Roman's eyes narrowed. "What?"

Toya slowly took a step toward her husband. "Roman I need to tell you the truth." Roman looked at his teary-eyed wife suspiciously.

"The truth about what?" he asked.

"My name is Toya Jenkins and I fabricated our relationship with lies to get to your finances," she admitted. "I lost my son to DCF because I was a prostitute and a junkie," Toya continued. She looked and pointed at Lorenzo. "I took the advice from my son's father, cleaned myself up at the same rehab institution where I met you." Roman was in shock and could not fathom what he was hearing.

"You were working there when I met you," Roman stated trying to gain clarity.

Toya shook her head slowly. "I was finishing up my community service." Roman clutched his chest as if his heart had been punctured or severely wounded. The woman he thought to be the love of his life and soul mate deliberately lied about everything to get to his wealth. Roman forced himself to speak but only responded with small whispers.

"I...saved myself...for you." Roman thought of their honeymoon and how he believed she was a virgin who vowed never to keep secrets. "How could you do this?" he asked trying to fight back tears of his own. Roman pulled out the same photos and crumpled up letter the officers at the hotel found. "So this was all really you the whole time." Their voices echoed through his head. *"How well do you know your wife?"* Roman cleared his throat and used his shirt to wipe tears from his eyes and then glared at Lorenzo. "So you're the father of her child?" he questioned.

Lorenzo took a deep breath. "I'm the reason for all this...don't blame her," Lorenzo pleaded. "I made her what she is today...I pimped her out on the street and she was my right hand when I was a dope boy," Lorenzo told him. "We grew up in the gutter and had to do whatever we had to if we wanted to survive," he explained. Lorenzo reached under his shirt and retrieved the firearm he had been carrying since he walked in the church. "If you want to punish someone then punish me...Toya deserves your forgiveness." Lorenzo knelt down and slid the firearm to Roman which stopped right before him. Toya was stunned at his words and actions and at the moment she knew without a doubt he was truly sincere. Even though Lorenzo was putting his life on the line to protect her she still had the small Beretta that detective Matthews had given her concealed in her clothes. Roman stared at the firearm that lay before him and slowly picked it up glaring at both Toya and Lorenzo. Although Roman was a spiritual man his flesh seemed to be getting the best of him.

"So it's up to me for you to get your son back," Roman said out loud. "After all you've done you don't deserve your son or forgiveness," he said angrily. Roman was compelled by his heartbreak and the feelings of hurt, betrayal, and the knowledge of being lied to. He raised the firearm and pulled the slide back aiming at Lorenzo's forehead.

The intercom beeped in. "Mr. Jacobson are you sure you want to do this? You claim to be a man of God. Do you think you're portraying the image of Christ right now?" Mr. Chess questioned. Lorenzo didn't show even an ounce of fear, even though he was looking directly down the barrel of a gun a few feet away from him. It seemed as though Roman had ignored the questions that Mr. Chess asked him as he placed his index finger on the trigger. Toya quickly pulled out the small Beretta she had concealed and pointed it at Roman. Her hand shook uncontrollably, unable to keep a steady aim at the fixed target.

"You would defend the man who put you through all this!" Roman yelled demanding to know. "I was the one who gave you everything! A home...the car of your dreams...and you betrayed me for him!" Roman was infuriated and could not hold back the feelings of revenge. He looked directly in Toya's teary eyes. "You're going to kill me for him? Why do you want him to live?" Toya lowered her weapon.

"Rome, I know you're hurt and upset and you have every right to be," she said in a soothing voice. "I didn't intentionally do this. I thought this was the only way I could get my son back," she continued. "The courts required me to provide steady income, successfully complete my community service hours, and remain off any drugs," she added. "With your help I could show the judge and DCF I was in a good position to raise my son. That's the truth." Roman was overwhelmed by the intense pain and hurt that had been inflicted upon him emotionally. It was too much to bear and he felt as though he was in anguish and torment. What Joyce did to him was excruciating and he honestly could not forgive her. In the heat of the moment he wanted vengeance and was willing to kill them both, but he could not bring himself to do it. He dropped the firearm and looked down in defeat.

"Are you able to forgive her of her transgression and what she has done to you?" Mr. Chess chimed over the intercom. Roman slowly raised his head and forced himself to look, teary eyed, upon his wife who reciprocated with tears in her eyes as well.

"I loved you with all of me...and you used me...lied to me... when you could've told me the truth...I would of easily helped you get your son," he explained with tears slowly falling. "I'm sorry, but I can never forgive you...the pain I feel is the pain you will feel as well." Roman turned and slowly walked out the door, leaving the two behind to deal with their problems. Toya watched in horror and disbelief as the only salvation for her son walked out the door.

"Wait!" she cried out as she chased after her husband. She turned the door handle but to her surprise the door was locked. Toya twisted and pulled at the doorknob but the door refused to be opened.

"Automated lock," the intercom interjected.

She fell to her knees in despair. "Please spare my son," she said whimpering.

The intercom came on. "I'm terribly sorry, Mrs. Jacobson. You're aware of the terms and conditions," Mr. Chess said flatly.

Toya wailed. "He's an innocent boy!" she cried out.

"An innocent boy who had to suffer as a result of your choices," Mr. Chess responded. Lorenzo, who had been quiet and motionless for some time, walked over toward Toya to console her. She rejected him immediately.

"No! Stay away from me. This is your fault!" she lashed out at him. "You need to do something to save your son!"

Lorenzo reluctantly backed away from Toya and looked at the screen that enabled them to watch their son who surprisingly was nowhere visible on the screen. "He's gone," Lorenzo said bewildered. The weeping Toya looked up at Lorenzo and followed his gaze toward the television monitor and realized what Lorenzo was referring to.

"Where is he!" she screamed. The intercom came on right after a noise was heard near the door Toya leaned against.

"It's open...your son is at the door," Mr. Chess said calmly. Toya quickly rose to her feet and flung the door open where her seven-year-old awaited patiently. She clutched the boy and hugged him tightly, refusing to let him go this time. Lorenzo wanted to interact with the boy but hesitated out of guilt for not being there from the beginning. Jeremiah tugged at his mother's hair to get her attention.

"Mommy, Mr. Chess told me to give this to you," he said. He handed his mom a small white envelope with the word "checkmate" on it. Puzzled, she ripped open the envelope and a piece fell to the floor. Toya knelt down and picked up the object that had fallen to the floor, which appeared to be the king chess piece. She heard a familiar locking noise that indicated that they were once again locked in. A clanking noise overhead forced both Toya and Lorenzo to look at the ceiling where they saw a ventilation airway opened. They stared at each other confused.

Toya instinctively held her son closely to her. Lorenzo sniffed the air and gagged after he took a deep breath. He began coughing and it seemed as though he were struggling to breathe as he clutched his chest.

"What is it?" Toya asked curiously.

Lorenzo fell to his knees and grabbed his throat. "I…can't…breathe."

Before she could respond, she inhaled the gas that apparently had been released from the vents. This gas pervaded the air quickly and it didn't long before Toya and young Jeremiah were writhing on the floor suffocating. Their eyes turned red from the lack of oxygen and the strain their body was enduring gasping and choking for air. Lorenzo slowly crawled toward Toya, and grabbed her hand and squeezed tightly. This naturally got Toya's attention and she glimpsed at her baby's father just in time to see him mouth the words, "I'm sorry." Toya was in no position to speak and could only comprehend the fact that her baby boy was dying all because of his parents' poor decisions. She would happily accept death if only he could have a chance to live and be better than his parents. After everything she'd done and planned, it really did come back to haunt and terrorize her. Toya squeezed Lorenzo's hand and clutched her son as tightly as possible as her heartbeat slowed down and would eventually come to permanent halt.

She whispered in her son's ear, which would be for the last time, "I…love…you." Toya's mind then thought about Roman and the pain she had caused him and understood truly why he could not forgive her. If he had, he would have been weakened and susceptible to more treachery. Toya knew this curse all too well because she had experienced it with Lorenzo which brought them inevitably to their last breath. "*I'm sorry, Roman*," she thought to herself. A loud banging noise came from the opposite side of the door that kept them locked in. Toya could barely hold on and saw a glimpse of the door being broken open. She witnessed Roman, firefighters, and the paramedic crew rush in just before she went unconscious...

10

FORMIDABLE OPPONENT

Doctors successfully revived Toya, who awoke in an intensive care hospital facility. Her vital signs and primary functions appeared to be working normally according to the medical equipment that showed the data. Her mind naturally processed only one thought.

"Jeremiah!" she yelled, panicking and grabbing at the IV tubes coming out of her body. Nurses quickly gathered around the frantic Toya trying to calm and reassure her.

"Ma'am...ma'am calm down! Everything is fine. Your son is safe." One of the nurses said.

"Where is he?" she asked in a concerned voice.

"Excuse me, nurses, I'll take it from here." A slightly familiar voice said. Toya looked and saw Nurse Greene walk over toward where she was bedridden. The nurse smiled as she sat near the edge of the bed. "Jeremiah is fine. He's on a respirator in a room down the hall, as well as his father." Toya sighed in relief, overjoyed that her son was safe and sound. Nurse Greene reached for Toya's hand and gently gave it a squeeze. "I have good news for you," she informed. Nurse Greene handed Toya a large white envelope that had her real name on it. "In that envelope are signed documents from Bishop Chess that allow you to have full parental rights and guardianship of your son." Toya winced and gasped at the name she just heard. "A check for one million dollars is also within the envelope," Nurse Greene said happily, with a huge smile across her face. Toya looked both astounded and confused.

"*Why would he do all this?*" she thought to herself. "I don't understand."

Nurse Greene rubbed Toya's hand soothingly. "Sssh…all you have to do is rest, dear. Everything is okay now." The nurse rose to her feet and exited the ICU room leaving Toya with a surreal feeling. After her near-death experience, suddenly all seemed perfectly well. Inevitably questions flooded her mind. "*How did we survive? Why did he let us go?*" She stared at the envelope that contained the million-dollar check. Roman obviously had forgiven her and granted her the finances for a secure future. After everything she put him through he still found it in his heart to do this unbelievable good deed. A tear rolled down her puffy face as she thought about her husband. She worried about his well-being and the consequences he may be dealt for sleeping with his own wife.

"I believe a thanks is an order." Toya had been too sedated and tranquil to be startled by the familiar voice. Out of the corner of the shadows walked her husband in an expensive navy blue suit with matching suede shoes. Roman took a seat near the edge of the bed and stared at his bride. Toya's eyes retreated. She was unable to face him, let alone look him in the eye. Roman chuckled, picking up on her body language. "Looks like you're in good hands for recovery," he said looking at her vital signs on the medical equipment.

"Roman...I am...so sorry," she said sincerely. She forced herself to meet his gaze and fear consumed her. He glared at her with pure contempt, absolute hate, and an evil that outmatched Mr. Chess.

"No you're not. Not yet," he replied through clenched teeth. Roman rose to his feet.

"You saved me though...you gave me this check," she reminded.

Roman nodded. "I didn't save you...someone intervened," he informed her. Roman took a step closer to the bed until his shadow covered her face. Toya stared up at him and saw his pearly whites as he flashed a malicious grin. "You think this over?" he questioned. Roman slowly removed his wedding ring off his left finger and placed it on the envelope beside her. "It won't end until death do us part, sweetheart." He leaned in and kissed the petrified Toya on her forehead. "I promise the games have only just begun," he whispered to her. Before allowing her to say anything, he left her alone in the hospital bed terrified. Roman quickly bypassed the nurses, doctors, and people present within the hospital. He made his way to his limousine and got comfortably seated inside.

"So how did it go?" Another passenger reading a newspaper accompanied Roman in the limo.

"It went well. So what's next, boss?" Roman asked. The passenger who sat across from Roman was concealed by the newspaper, but now revealed his face. The elder in a jet-black, striped suit, Mr. Chess, handed Roman the newspaper. Roman took the newspaper and read the headline about a mysterious masked vigilante who saved another helpless victim yet again. "He's the one who intervened," Roman said.

The elder nodded. "He's also the next *competitor*. We have a lot of work to do, Mr. Jacobson," Mr. Chess replied. The limo sped from the curb quickly, leaving the hospital behind and heading to their next destination. *"This one may be a worthy opponent,"* Mr. Chess thought to himself with a malicious smirk on his face.

THE END
We shall play again

About the Author

Khaliyl Adisa is a certified personal trainer, registered amateur boxer, and founder of Torture Training Exercises. He became a certified personal trainer in 2011 at the World Fitness Association in Ft. Lauderdale, Florida, under Nick Tansey. Along with his passion for fitness, Khaliyl also pursues combat sports and currently trains in boxing under Tito Ocasio at the John 3:16 & 17 Boxing Gym.

As a means to help his community, Khaliyl established Torture Training to push individuals out of their mediocre, sedentary lifestyles and into fit, driven, and hardworking men and women in his city. Aside from training, he has discovered a love for writing and has plans to write more books in various genres.

Made in the USA
Lexington, KY
25 August 2018